Face **IT**

(*Bewitching Stories of Human Onions*)

Face IT

Bewitching Stories of Human Onions

written by
SMIEETAA

ADHYYAN BOOKS

FaceIT

1st Edition

All rights reserved

Publication Date: February 2019

Price: ₹300 | $11.99

ISBN: 978-93-88644-08-2

Published by:

Adhyyan Books

Office No. 637,

Opposite Vivanta by Taj,

DDA SFS. Pocket-1, Dwarka,

Sec-22, New Delhi-110077

Website: http://adhyyanbooks.com

E-mail: contact@adhyyanbooks.com

Edited by:

Amrita Bakshi, Phillipines

Amritabakshi3010@gmail.com

To Chandrashekar and Shekar Pulekar, who gave
me the opportunity to be a part of the IT industry!

To all the organizations I have worked for,
my mentors and my colleagues!
&
My parents who dreamt big!

!!! SHRI GANESH!!!

"There is nothing like a low performer or a high performer,
Performer is someone who is good at something.
He/she becomes a low performer if the person
evaluating cannot use his/her Skillset."

-Anonymous

Acknowledgement

I remember writing a script for a play to be performed at the Alumni meet in my college, that is how "Smruti" who was 2 years junior to me in my college got introduced to my writing skills. Later on, I referred Smruti to one of the organizations I worked for. Till then, I had bolstered the experience of 4 years in the industry and she was a fresher. When I and Smruti worked in the same organization, she became a part of my dabba group and we used to have fun during our lunch times. Sharing our work experience, gossips and being observant about the surroundings was the time when Smruti suggested me to write a book on these experiences. I was not sure until the year 2009, when something clicked and I started writing. This book cannot go without a "thank you" to her.

I kept adding the content, until one day something happened again and I decided to recast my experiences in this book. Being a Social media addict, I posted my feeling and guess what? Almost everybody wanted to read it, which is what motivated me. The comments kept flowing and the motivation to complete the book went on a high. Thanks to all my friends, colleagues and family who trusted me for being creative.

In another week's time, I received an invite from Adhyyan books for a "Workshop on how to write a book". I felt 'this is the time the book should go online rather than remain lifeless in a draft stage'. I attended the workshop mentored by Nitin Soni, I was convinced, influenced and all my anxieties were cleared off. A BIG thanks to Nitin and his team for working out with me.

The cartoons in the book are done by Ghanshyam Deshmukh ("Bolakya resha" fame). Thanks to him for accepting my request for creating cartoons and coming up with the same in a stint. I told him all the stories just once, and he came back with the cartoons promptly. I would let the pictures talk for him.

Thanks to my friends Ranjeet Deshmukh, Nitin Madan and my husband Sudeep Raikar, who played the roles of "DEVIL'S ADVOCATE". They made sure that I pour in the best of me. Gratitude to my Son; Swaraj who patiently let me do what I wanted to and kept on asking me stories from my book.

Thanks to the entire IT industry, which gives me my bread and butter. I hold very high respect for my work, the organizations I have had worked for and the people I have had worked with. Having said that, I find myself extremely fortunate to be a part of the industry, which is taking the nation from just a labor potential to skilled-labor potential country.

Introduction

The heat was rising! Pune summer was not as torturous as I felt it this year. Not just me, but everybody else in the team too could feel the waves of the piping hot weather. Everybody was sweating. The reason was not summer alone, nor was some hot celebrity visiting our campus. It was the "Appraisal* time".

*[Appraisal; a process which rates how one performed. Theoretically, Appraisal means "appraising self/proving yourself" or from the employer's perspective, it is "evaluating the employee"]. Primarily one (employee) is evaluated on the performance basis and there are many criterions to evaluate the same. As a matter of fact it also depends on who is evaluating.

I hated this time of the year and I believe everybody working in IT hates it too. "We slog throughout the entire year, and guess what? At the end of the year, we need to reprove it to our boss. Prove it! Prove what?" asked one of the new comers. I remember one of a discussion on the chai tapari (tea stall corner) where the agenda of a group was "what does the boss do throughout the year?" And these were some of the thoughts: 'Stock market—how much would one invest? Social networking—how much....? Games—may be at that time of the day when the sugar level in the body is high! Meetings---don't they get bored talking about the same thing and looking at the same graphs with different colors?' That discussion did not end there, but it would be better if I stop here or I might let many cats out of the bag!!

All of a sudden everybody around started talking about goals, 1-1(one to one), BE-ME-AE (Below-Met-Above—Expectation) and "%". People around me started turning as best friends or colleagues. Well there is a difference between a "friend" and "colleague". Believe me or not but this is the time when we are able to demark a person as a friend or a colleague. Though it is re-iterated that "the appraisal process is confidential" yet everybody discusses it with someone or the other (This is a normal human behavior). So those who share the information fall in 'friend' category and rest as 'colleague'. Hold on! This does not end here, we are going to talk about one more category and they are by far known as "*PERFORMER". Did you read it as "STAR PERFORMER"? Star performer; the brightest in team and supposedly the person who performs above expectation, the one who is ranked as number 1 in the team after the Appraisal and the one who takes away the major portion of the cake (budget). The one whom the boss will introduce as a "star performer" to a new comer in the organization and in short tell him "it won't work for you".

The remaining members of the team, including me, would keep guessing "what makes him/her the Star performer?" This thought of mine gave birth to a keeda (Hindi word for a germ) "Star performer". I started thinking about and observing every "performer" I met in my 16 years of IT experience. This book is all about my understanding of the mechanics behind them being a 'Star performer'. It is not the bright shining star I am taking about in this volume. They are "*" (*Terms and condition apply) kind of a people.

While observing all these "*performers", I realized that they exhibit a specific attribute called as human behavior. My interest in human psychology and recent trainings I went through helped me more to comprehend. People (@ work) wear different masks (not being their true self), go out of the humanity square and pull themselves in the sweatshops that are run. That might not be their true self. They may behave entirely different when at the workplace. They exploit themselves; at times others too and jump over the fence to prove themselves. Some kind of layers While I am thinking of printing another volume to talk about the real stars, I want to begin with the grey layers of human beings. Based on understanding, observation and personal interpretation, I have created the characters in this book. So though some of these characters might appear sitting next to you in your office, they are truly fictitious. **Any resemblance is purely coincidental...**

PS: This book can be read for awareness of the characters that exist @work place. The book does not provide solution, but awareness helps, isn't?

"Awareness is empowering."

—*Rita Wilson*

Contents

CHAPTER
One

*"Hiring people is an art, not a science and
Resumes can't tell whether someone will fit in the culture."*

-Howard Schultz *(Chairman-Starbucks)**

S he was fair, zero-figured, stylish and had a cute face. At the reception she said "my name is **Sneha** and I have come for an interview".

"Please have a seat." said the receptionist as she was amidst something. Sneha sat on the sofa in the reception area, next to few other girls. Two girls out of the group murmured amongst them:

Girl1: "She should put on some weight, she looks like a victim of malnutrition."

Girl2: "She is smart and has good communication skills. See, all the boys are looking at her."

Sneha looked at them as she could spy-hear what was going on. She passed them annoyed looks and dropped her head back on her mobile screen, pushing them and creating some more space for her on the sofa. The "sofa" was donated by the GM's wife! Every festive season, his wife would change the interiors of her house and the office reception would get a new sofa. Of course, it is a workplace not a dump yard! Recycling is good anyways. This happens in smaller organizations. In bigger organizations, everything needs a Purchase Order and it has to be the "State of Art".

Reception area is small, and no internal operations can be traced from here. All the freshers (job seekers) kept looking at the doors which opened into the floor area. Whenever somebody swiped the card, the machine made a typical noise and everybody tried to peep in. While everybody was busy peeping in, the recruiter leading the hiring drive walked in. He escorted all the freshers to a bigger training room called **"Chameli"**, which was at the far end of the office. As they all were walking through the passage, they realized that all the conference rooms were named on flowers. Conference rooms are supposed to be a place where meetings, trainings and conferences are arranged. But they could be used for mass conspiracy as well.

"We have all the conference rooms on one side of the floor and the bays on other side." informed the recruiter to the freshers. Somebody from the group asked the recruiter "Sorry, but what a bay is?" The recruiter quite enthusiastically replied, "Bays are narrowed-down office spaces or rather shared office spaces. The bay consists of cubicles. Cubicle is an Individual's workspace. The cubicles are built such that the person sitting inside can concentrate on work and has enough privacy."

All the eyes were rolling on the name plates, the stylish monitors, and personalized work spaces. The common areas had big sofas and interesting concepts. The walls had pictures of the products the company manufactured, some of the team pictures and some motivational quotes. To freshers, everything was amazing as it looked spic and span. Everybody was feeling cozy with that centralized air conditioner blowing, maintained at the correct temperature. No heat and no dust.

"Those who wish to use the washrooms please do so now as we get started with written exams in another 10 minutes." said the recruiter. All of them paraded on the work floor, trying to locate the restrooms until one of the team member from recruiting team directed them. Since it was just beginning of the day, the entire office was empty. Few early birds were on their seats though. They were watching and remembering their days as freshers. As soon as they spotted Sneha with the recruiter, they kept staring at Sneha with their dropping jaws.

All the freshers settled in the training room. Soon the recruiters handed the question paper to all of them. "Excuse me. Can I get a pen? I forgot mine." said one of the freshers. "Sure, anybody else needs any other stationary?

Please feel free to ask." replied the recruiter. Further the recruiter informed the freshers that there was a common question paper set for all the streams.

Every September-October time frame, most of the organizations hire some freshers (fresh graduates from College). They hire freshers for fresh ideas, some fresh energy in the team since freshers can work the most. Moreover, freshers are like sponge, they can soak more as compared to an experienced person and are easy to mold. People inside the organization, look at freshers for "clean and clearer faces" as it gets one out of the mundane.

As soon as the exam was done, the batch was asked to move in an open common area. This place had huge sofa with a huge TV set and some books in the shelf nailed to the wall. Sneha was seesawing from one corner to other as she was talking on phone with somebody. All men in the office were gazing at her as nobody in the office ever dressed the way she had on her interview day. She was wearing a black short skirt (Levis, everyone could read it because it was a low waste) and a pink color (Babe) top. She had worn silver color sandal. The ones slightly older in the industry would not have dared to wear that kind of attire on the very first interview, in spite of the fact that nobody belonged to Chanakya's era...

It was not just her, almost all the freshers were wearing all colors; red, yellow and fluorescent green which otherwise nobody in the office would wear. That is what made the office vibrant on the hiring day. They had worn all sort of funky clothes as they all seemed to be highly inspired by their Bollywood favorites. Sneha was inspired by the youngest actress in Bollywood! Besides she carried an Apple iPhone! Everybody was wondering how could she or for that matter anyone who had just come out of the college, afford to have an iPhone. It is an expensive phone for college pass outs. It is supposedly flaunted by higher designation bosses. May be it is the generation gap that is making them embellish it!

Normally, the scene that makes an appearance in case of fresher interviews is nervous faces, people with lot of books and notes around, some chanting beads and some visiting the restrooms frequently. However, this batch was slightly different as everyone was busy with their digital devices. Sneha too was playing some games on her handset while others were constantly chatting. It was apparent from the WhatsApp audible key tones. All of them had missed reading the warning "Keep your mobile on silent while on work floor", which is why an official from the floor reminded them.

The recruiter walked out of the conference room to announce the names of the selected candidates. Sadly, only 6 were selected out of a batch of 60 people. And Sneha was one of them. "Congratulations guys! You are the lucky 6. All the best for your face-to-face discussion! Please be seated while we call out for you" said the recruiter. For freshers, the face-to-face round is very critical as they are judged on a lot of parameters in this round. Learning ability, analytical skills and general attitude are the skills on which they are evaluated. On the basis of marks they scored in their technical rounds, they were lined up. Sneha was the last one to go. As the interviews were progressing, she was getting restless; constantly chatting with someone. "Can you put your mobile on silent mode please" requested the receptionist to Sneha. She slipped her mobile in the pocket of her skirt and started looking around. After a few minutes, one of the members from the interview panel came out and announced Sneha's name. It was her turn to step in the interview room.

Sneha: Hello everyone.

Amit and the second interviewer: Hi Sneha, please have a seat.

Amit: How are you? How has been your experience with the process so far?

Sneha: It has been good so far.

Amit: So how many steps did you take to reach this office?

Sneha: I took the lift from basement-1.

Amit: Ok. Can you solve the given puzzle? Please tell me if you already know.

Sneha looked at Amit, smiled and attempted the puzzle. She solved the puzzled in about 3-4 minutes, which supposedly was amazing as per Amit.

Amit: Why should we hire you?

Sneha: I believe I am the last choice as almost all my other friends have already left and I don't think that they were able to crack the game.

Just to make her talk more, the two interviewers pitch some more questions.

Amit: Which was your favorite subject Sneha?

Sneha: Umm... I liked all of them. But my favorite during entire Engineering course was engineering drawing.

Second interviewer: Why? Looks like you love drawing!

Sneha: Well, I definitely love drawing. But I had a crush on my Graphics teacher.

Second interviewer: Interesting! But he must be quite older to you.

Sneha: Yes he is. But it was just a crush. I never wanted to marry him.

Amit smiled and informed her that the HR would get back to her. On that she said, "Is it so hard a decision to make? Can't you tell me now?" Amit and the other interviewer were spell-bound for a moment. Amit said, "We have to follow certain protocol and cannot disclose the same now. Don't worry, you will come to know if your name shows in 'hired'." She left the room with a big smile on her face assuming that she was hired.

While writing the feedback for her, other interviewer asked Amit, "So what's your take?" Amit replied, "She is technically ok, she will need a lot of time to grasp things, she has a swag (negative one), but she is smart. She is glamorous." He asked to comment in the feedback form as **"we should hire her"**.

The same was communicated to the hiring team* (*The hiring team is responsible for carrying out the entire process right from filtering the resume, checking with the candidates if they are interested in being interviewed, setting up the panel for interview, collecting the feedback, and signing an offer letter). Of course, the offers are decided by the Business unit head or the manager who is hiring the candidate. In this case, it was Amit. Processes apart, hiring depends on the destiny and luck as well. So many deserving candidates get rejected for some trivial reasons and candidates not fitting requirements get hired for some hot positions. Some candidates get rejected because of conflicts between the hiring team and interviewers or conflicts between the interviewers. In spite of some negative comments from the HR, and other managers about her attitude, Sneha was hired. As Amit had a bigger say!

"She will add a lot of glamour and become a motivation. Also, we should hire other five freshers too. Who will waste time in these interview processes? It is better we hire what we have right now; mold them the way we want. Whoever performs well, will be absorbed any which ways."

said Amit. The statement "she is glamorous" travelled faster than the light and hit every cube in the office. "Amit should not have used that word even if it was an informal forum for discussion." said Supriya. Supriya, was part of Amit's team. Nevertheless, Sneha along with others was hired. Most of the men in the team were happier about her hiring news than the one who referred her. Everybody now was looking forward to her joining date.

CHAPTER
Two

"First things First!"

"A VERY WARM WELCOME"

—Sneha Godbole,
Rimsha Chaterjee,
Kavitha S,
Sameer Deodhar &
Imran Kadri.

Whenever, somebody new joined, the reception area would have bouquets, sweets and the display board with the Welcome note for the new hires. The reporting time on joining date by default is 9.30 in morning. Almost everybody was on time, except Kavitha who was travelling from Tamil Nadu to Pune. It seemed she had communicated the same to the HR team. Kavitha's husband had been working in the same company for a year now. He had recently married Kavitha who was 5 years younger to him. She was studying when they got married. Her husband referred ("Referral with a strong jack") her as a fresher and that is how she got in.

Generally on the first/joining day everybody is treated very specially. Rather that is the only day when one is treated specially. Sameer, Rimsha and Imran reached office half an hour early. Sneha was on time; sharp 9.30 AM. Sneha wore a black trouser and a linen white shirt. It was slightly transparent and showed off her pink bra. She looked extremely stylish as she did in her interview. The black nail paint looked good too. Her bold eyeliner and postal red lipstick highlighted her features grandly. Hair tucked with a small pin. While everybody was settling down with their documents in one hand and bouquets in other, Kavitha arrived with a big red color luggage bag. It seemed she had come directly from the railway station. Curly hair, slightly dark complexion and straight nose were the marked features. While adjusting her spectacle, she asked the receptionist, "Hey, can I too get that the bouquet ?" "Oh you will get one for sure." said the receptionist and smiled. "Please be seated for a while, as you might be tired Kavitha." continued the receptionist.

Imran was in his formals and Sameer had worn jeans with a T-shirt. "Good morning everyone! Glad to see you all here. You all are looking fresh and excited. Adding to that excitement; today there will be no work and only play." informed the HR. "We will be introducing you to all the processes, places and people. All three are important to get started. Once we are done, we will hand you over to your respective Managers." said another HR. The entire

Human Resource teams mostly consist of women and few men. Most of them, in fact all of them, are good looking, and well-groomed. The HR took almost half a day to explain the process, places and handed over the new hires to their respective managers for new hires to know the people they will be working with.

"Hey Amit Sir, glad to see you again. BTW, that's a cool shirt." said Sneha to Amit. This was the first time ever Amit was getting complimented. "What brand is it?" asked Sneha. "Oh glad you liked it", reacted Amit while trying to locate the brand tag on his sleeves, and front pocket. "I have not noticed the brand but I got it from the United States for $199." "Oh that's way expensive. Let me check which brand that is." said Sneha while trying to peep through Amit's shirt's collar. While controlling all his excitement Amit replied, "Indeed it is. By the way, in our office nobody is addressed as "SIR" OR "MADAM", we all believe in flat hierarchy. Anyways, let me introduce you all to the rest of my team."

Amit introduced all the new hires to his team mates. He kept looking at Sneha when she said, "Hello, I am Sneha, Sneha Godbole (Bond, James bond type)." One common thing that everybody observed while she was getting introduced was she carried a big artificial smile which enhanced her dimples. The boys, who were a part of the same team as Sneha, blushed when she smiled at them. Rimsha who was hired in the same team was rated as ok types (well there are a lot of 'types') as she appeared dumb. Sameer, an IIT pass out was hired too. He was very confident and dynamic. He was moving around the office on his own and had already got himself introduced to the office before the HR would do the honors. This was the first team which had a lot of diversity. And during all of this, Amit forgot to introduce Imran. Although, Imran did make efforts to introduce himself to others but nobody showed any interest.

A tradition in IT is, every new hire is assigned a buddy (a mentor). Moreover, these new hires get distributed across the teams. So all the new hires who had joined, got distributed in various teams. Each of them had a different buddy. The manager-"Amit" insisted to buddy with Sneha. So distribution and assignment of resources is also based on CHOICE. One prefers to buddy with the person one likes. It is not mutual though.

It all depends on the processes that an organization may have. It varies from organization to organization. Some new hires are walked through an induction program or some sort of training which might give insight about the organization. In some organizations, they make the new hires work from day-1. This also depends on the manager's interest and requirement in the team. If there is less workload, they might as well spend time learning something new. If not, then they have to work. This batch was a lucky one as their joining dates coincided with a celebration and offsite week* (*Offsite is an annual outing which is sponsored by the company. All the expenses are borne by the organization, everything; the travel, food and accommodation. The employees are put up in the best hotel and taken to the best place (based on the budget)). This time the entire office was going to GOA. Generally

Amit would assign work to new hires on the first day itself. But this time, Amit was checking with the new hires if they were interested in joining the trip in spite of the fact that all arrangements were made. All of them exclaimed, "Why not?"

It was slightly difficult to convince the organizing committee, but Amit used all his influence to include the new hires in his team for the offsite. Everybody in the office was surprised; as this was the first time he himself was going for some offsite. He was attracted to Sneha. Although, all the men were but Amit's face and behavior showed it all. It was a welcoming change. "Train journey would be fun Amit. You should join us!" said Supriya. Amit in his accent, "Well, I don't think I really need to waste all that time." Amit had booked flight tickets for himself (@organization's cost) to avoid wastage of time in train travel.

CHAPTER
Three

*"We didn't realize we were creating memories,
We were just having fun."*

-Anonymous

Everything was planned. Train tickets were booked, and hotel accommodation was finalized, may it be the pickup from employee's home for the railway station or seats in the train. Almost 3 bogies were booked for the entire office. Hotel rooms and room sharing was arranged. The entire Fun committee was running around and everyone was impressed by the efforts they were taking to make trip interesting. Entire office received emails on "What to do/not to do", "What to wear/what to avoid", "What to carry/avoid" and "how to behave" from the fun committee. Nobody in the team was allowed to carry their laptop.

Finally, it was Thursday evening when everybody gathered in the office with their luggage for the 3 day stay. Yes, it was an offsite for 4.5 days; two working days and one weekend. After completing their work on Thursday, the team started with their journey. The ritual of cracking a coconut and squeezing the lemon before the journey begins is an inevitable part of any travel. Having completed that, the buses started and navigated to the railway station.

It was a pleasant evening as the Sun was still setting. Almost an hour was left for the train to depart. Everybody was enjoying, looking around, buying mineral water or magazines. Kavitha was sticking to her husband. As if she was going for her second honeymoon☺ . This is the advantage of working in the same organization. Of course, it has disadvantages too. The train departed on the scheduled time. The fun committee requested everybody to settle in the train first and then sort out the seat numbers as they always knew that people would settle as per their choice and group of people.

All the new girls joined the "mahila mandal (as the ladies in organization named it)". No matter how hard diversity is stressed and lobbies are avoided, yet there will always be a 'ladies only' or 'men only' group in any organization. Nobody creates them, they happen by default. There were about 20-30 women in a team of 120 people. And most of them were a part of this gang (exceptions were there). Few of them had dropped the offsite as they had their children and family to take care of. Some organizations do allow families for annual offsite, it all depends on the budget.

Rimsha and Sneha were good friends by now. They were enjoying all the jokes and gossips the ladies were sharing. "You should avoid make-up every day. That damages the skin." said Supriya to Sneha. Sneha, looked at her and smiled. "Looks like Aunty is too concerned for me." murmured Sneha to Rimsha. Supriya continued, "By the way, why do you girls wear such clothes to office, you are out of college now." Both Rimsha and Sneha looked at Supriya who was, kind of, leading the topic in that group and everybody else was giggling. "Leave it to them Suppu. Let them live their own way." said another lady to Supriya. "Don't forget your good old days Suppu." Supriya; the leader of Mahila mandal group. She hated everybody for some or the other reason. Yet she had good relation with everyone and was known for her gossiping nature. Rimsha and Sneha were getting bored by the entire conversation and wanted to leave. Sneha gathered all the courage to say "Good night" and both moved to their allocated seats. Supriya said "Well, good night for now, but there is no other group to accommodate you." She laughed and everybody else joined her. Both the new girls were not able to relate.

The train was picking up its speed and everybody could hear the whistles blow. Everybody on the Konkan Kanya express was flabbergasted to see the scenic beauty in the starry night. Sneha and Rimsha stood near the doors watching the countryside passing by. Amidst all the noises, they could hear somebody playing guitar. They started looking out for the person when they finally found a group of men and women singing songs. Both Rimsha and Sneha asked, if they could join them. The entire group was all eager to have them in their company. Few of the members from this group were part of Fun committee and appeared very interesting. Sameer who had joined with Rimsha and Sneha was also part of this group. He was a professional guitarist. Music was his passion. Rimsha and Sneha did not know about this, as Sameer did not broadcast it to everyone. In his orientation, Sameer had mentioned to HR that he wanted to join a music group (if one existed). HR then introduced him to the funtoosh group. The fun committee had lot of chaps who were incredible musicians, specialized in multitasking and technically sound folks. Sneha realized that the entire group was wearing the T-shirt with a tagline **"Fun (toosh) KO seriously lo"**. They had designed these T-shirts for themselves. She was very impressed and complimented "Hey those T-shirts are cool! What is this "funtoosh"?" "You want one?" asked Sameer.

"Well, I don't mind." replied Sneha. Sameer who was extremely notorious, stood up and removed his T-shirt. "Take this." said Sameer. Sneha blushed and so did Rimsha. "Yuk... Please, I don't want this, not sure if you ever washed it." said Sneha. "C'mon, why would I wash a new t-shirt, crazy women? By the way funtoosh is the name of our fun committee." replied Sameer a.k.a SAM. Sameer was 6 feet one inch tall, handsome features, pleasant countenance and extremely agreeable. He had a little pony and a dense well-groomed beard. He almost looked like 'Ritesh in Banjo' movie. He slipped in his T-shirt and went for a smoke with another boy from the group. Rest of the folks continued with their singing. It was almost 2.00 AM. Everybody in the team was hungry. They had few dinner boxes that they carried with them, they thought of uncapping the same. They distributed the same amongst themselves and checked with the girls if they wanted to munch. "We are stuffed. Thanks for asking." said Sneha.

Meanwhile Sameer returned with his friend and sat with his guitar. "Hey why don't you girls sing a song?" asked somebody. "Well NO, I can't sing." replied Sneha while looking at Rimsha. Rimsha was a little hesitant too but Sameer said, "Rimsha I know you can sing and you like it too." "I will try." said Rimsha. Rimsha had learnt classical singing from her Mother who was a graduate in music. Rimsha had mentioned about this in her introduction which Sam recollected. Rimsha discussed a few things with Sameer and said "This is one of my favorite Hindi songs. It is from the movie "Parichay" and based on Raaga Yaman Kalyan. I hope you like it as I have not really practiced for some time now." Everybody cheered for her, and she started singing "Biti na bitaye raina...." Everybody got completely lost in her melodious and sweet voice until a mobile ring created ripples. It was Sneha's mobile. Sneha walked out with her mobile, while Rimsha continued to sing.

"Why are you still awake?" asked Sneha to the other person on call. Everybody assumed that it would be her boyfriend as no other person would call at 2.45 AM☺. "People, let us take a power nap as we would be in GOA in another 4 hours' time." said one of the Team leads. Almost everybody was feeling sleepy now. They applauded for Rimsha. Rimsha thanked everyone and moved to her allocated seat. Sneha returned to the seat after half an hour. Rimsha had slept by then. Sneha kept typing on her mobile and went off to sleep.

The cold gust with the chirping of birds amidst the whistles of train was awe-inspiring. "Chai garam chai" bellowed the chai walla (The person who sells tea). That waked up almost everyone. The fun committee had arranged for early morning "CHAI (tea)" and some light snacks for the entire team. It was still an hour left to reach GOA. Few of the members were in queues outside the toilets, few of them brushing and some were still sleeping. The train was about to reach "Madgaon" station, when all the seniors and the fun committee team members asked everyone to pack up their belonging as it was time to get down the train.

"When are the buses arriving?" asked Supriya to the funtoosh team. "They will be here soon Supriya, please have patience." came the reply "What patience? It was such a pathetic journey, I could not sleep for the entire night." responded Supriya. Rest of the ladies looked at her, as she was the only person snoring in the entire compartment ☺. However, she was ignored. After 10-15 minutes, 3 posh AC buses arrived and everybody started their travel to the hotel booked for them. The stay arrangement for the entire team was made in a 5 star hotel; one of the best, and the one which had a private beach.

"Welcome Sir, Welcome mam!" greeted the staff members of hotel. They welcomed the team with colorful garlands, and hats. The staff served everyone fresh coconut water as the welcome drink.

Funtoosh allotted the rooms amongst members based on their choices. Rimsha and Sneha opted to share their rooms with the ladies from the Funtoosh team as they were loath to be a part of the Mahila Mandal. The hotel had allocated almost 40 cottages, and around 15 double rooms. The cottages were sea-facing and had a spectacular view. The Funtoosh team distributed printouts of the plan for the next two days. Everybody committed oneself to rest as the travel had made everyone a little frenzied. They were supposed to meet for lunch after which they had planned for some exaggerated activities.

The cottage that the new girls were allocated was very close to the sea and they could hear the waves amid all the noise while walking towards the cottage. They were allocated Cottage-204. It was beautiful; simply charming. Kavitha was also supposed to share the cottage with them just for the sake of process. "I am going to sleep." said Sneha to Rimsha. "Same here." replied Rimsha. Kavitha opened the door and they all were overwhelmed as the cottage had a living room, two bedrooms and a small balcony, which was like 250 meters away from the beach. The cottage was fastidiously designed and decorated. Every bedroom had a bathroom with a bathtub. The living area had a huge sofa and a center table decorated with local flowers. The hotel staff had spruced up with some "plum cake" and a bottle of "wine" on the center table. This was the first time ever when all the new girls were experiencing this kind of luxury. They surveyed the bedroom, which had a big Queen Size bed with a typical citrus fragrance. All of them crashed on the same bed and said "OH MY GOD, this is so amazing!" Rimsha got up, walked to the balcony and called the other two. "IT IS SO BEAUTIFUL!"

Rimsha started crying. She could not control herself. "Are you alright?" asked Kavitha and Sneha. Rimsha wiped off her tears and replied that she was fine. Kavitha offered her water and asked "What happened, why are you crying?" in her accent. "Are you missing your family?" "Yes! I am very happy and I feel that I am so lucky to work with such a great organization that treats the employees so well. I wish my parents were here." replied Rimsha. "Oh yes we all are fortunate. Now stop crying, let us all take some rest otherwise we all might fall sick and enjoy nothing." said Sneha. When they were changing, Kavitha realized that she had got her husband's bag and he had taken hers. She called him on the intercom and he came in no time. He left saying something in their native language, which the other two girls did not understand. "Kavitha, why don't you and your husband stay in the cottage, that will be so romantic?" asked Sneha. "I know, but that can't happen Na as that is not allowed Na." replied Kavitha.

"Girls, let us go to the beach in the evening." said Vidya who just checked in the room when all of them were changing. "By the way, my name is Vidya and I have been with the organization for more than 5 years. I am part of the funtoosh team and I shall be sharing the room with you." The girls introduced themselves to Vidya. "So are you part of Amit's team?" asked Sneha. "Thank fully not." replied Vidya. Sneha and Rimsha looked at each other. "Girls you will get to know a lot. As of now let us take rest. Will catch you in the evening." said Vidya. "That's great idea." replied all while diving in the bed. Nobody had lunch that day, as everybody was knocked out after the overnight journey.

The intercom kept ringing until Kavitha woke up and answered the call. She realized it was 7.30 PM in the evening. The funtoosh team called on the intercom to remind them of that day's celebration. "Girls, awake up na, Sneha, Rimsha ... Amma please wake up." shouted Kavitha. "Let me sleep, I am not going anywhere." said Rimsha. "What? It is so dark outside? Why did you not wake us all?" shouted Sneha. "I too was sleeping, the funtoosh team called Na for celebrations. Let us go amma." said Kavitha. Both Kavitha and Sneha rushed to the washroom. They were dressing up when they heard Vidya from the funtoosh team puking. Both of them rushed to check what was happening. "Are you ok?" asked

Sneha. "Well, yes. But looks like I am having acidity. You girls enjoy, I too will rest with Rimsha here."

"Sneha, you look so beautiful in this dress." said Kavitha. Sneha wore a black short skirt with white sleeveless top on it, whereas Kavitha was wearing a yellow and green salwar-kurta which was of anarkali style. "Where do you buy your dresses from, please take me next time along with you Na." said Kavitha. "Thank you so much and sure I shall take you." replied Sneha ignoring the question: where did she get her dress from. They both reached the banquet hall where the dinner and a small celebration were arranged. The dinner menu was outlandish. Everybody complimented Sneha for her looks and she was admired for rest of the evening.

The Funtoosh team had arranged for few events like musical chair, and Pictionary. Sameer heaved all his batch mates and made sure that everyone partook. The team did not continue the celebrations for long as they had bigger plans for the next day. However, they did announce the agenda for next day which included some site-seeing and a big party with some contests. Girls went back to the cottage and checked with Rimsha if she needed anything. She was sleeping and so was Vidya. Both Kavitha and Sneha sat in the balcony for some time without speaking a word.

Next day, all four of them woke up early and took a nice walk along the beach. They took some selfies and had lots of fun. Everybody from the team seemed refreshed as everybody was looking great with their vacation apparels, and ready-to-travel attitude when on the breakfast table. Everybody was ready for the site seeing. Goa site seeing is mostly about traveling from one beach to another and Goa shopping is all about bottles. The hotel had provided a tour guide and few buses for the same.

Everybody carried their DSLRs. Almost every IT professional has a DSLR, irrespective of him being a professional photographer or not. Since the boom of IT in India, if anything has grown apart from the real estate market is the growth in sales of DSLR cameras. Almost all the photographers were trying to have at least one picture of Sneha as she looked glamorous in her fluorescent green hot pant paired with a floral top. Her sunglasses summed it all.

"Hey Amit, when did you arrive?" asked Sneha after seeing Amit. "I arrived last night 11 PM. I took the flight after attending my conference call*." replied Amit. That conference call information was not asked for, but there were few more people around Sneha which is why he insisted on the same. (*Conference calls are the means to collaborate if the teams are distributed in various cities or states or countries. Most of the times, these calls are scheduled late in evenings or mid-nights. It is optional to attend these calls (unless one has an update), but it is at the discretion of an individual.) People like Amit attend it to reflect the impression of a workaholic person. The buses arrived and everybody moved in the buses. Amit sat alongside Sneha.

Amit was wearing his red-black striped T-shirt and beige color shorts. His big belly was frowning out while he sat. He was wearing his formal black shoes and white socks. Sneha looked at him and smiled. Amit noticed it and asked "Why are you smiling?" Sneha replied, "Who does the styling for you?" Amit was now a little conscious. "Why, is there something wrong?" asked Amit. "You need a lot of improvement. Nobody wears formal shoes on shorts and that too when one knows that they will be visiting a beach." replied Sneha while laughing loud. "That's true, but I took the flight right after office and packed whatever I could in hurry." said Amit. They discussed more about styling to conclude that Sneha will help Amit pick the right stuff once they are back in Pune.

Rimsha was mostly with the Funtoosh group as she could easily connect with them. Besides, she was left alone, as Sneha was with Amit and Kavitha with her husband. She preferred Sam's company. The funtoosh team had carried volleyball and the cricket kit for everybody to play on the beaches. After seeing a couple of beaches, the entire team decided to halt at Anjuna beach until the sunset. Few of the team members decided to rest, those left with some energy started playing and the girls went shopping with a plan to return before the sunset.

Everything had slowed down except the sea-waves. It

seemed as if they were running to clasp the setting sun. Charcoal dark figures moving around. And everything getting chiller. While everybody was posing with their cameras, Imran had got his water-colors and canvas. His canvas was merging well in that evening; perfect conclusion for any day. After couple of team pictures, everybody was asked to move immediately into the bus for the party that was lined up.

Sweaty and tired, everybody reached the hotel to see a very warm welcome message "Let's party hard". The funtoosh team informed everybody to return to the banquet hall around 7.30 PM for the grand party. The banquet hall had a stage set up with a bewildering backdrop and colorful lights. The team had planned for some dance performances, some music and some more surprises. The dress code for the day was "red and black". This was informed to the team before they left Pune so that they could carry the required party wear. The funtoosh team members were wearing blue denims with their peculiar black T-shirt and badge to demark themselves from others. They were wearing beautiful red hats, the typical Goan hat.

The mahila mandal had bought similar party gowns with identical accessories. The entire group was standing out in the crowd and all the ladies looked awesome. The theme for them was decided by Supriya who had curled her hair for this occasion. Most of the guys had worn shimmery red color shirt and black jeans combination.

The compère started the ceremony by welcoming everybody. She briefed about the entire event and contest. She also informed that everybody was supposed to collect their 3 coupons to avail hard drinks apart from the unlimited dinner and mock tails. That created a chaos as everyone rushed to the counter which was giving out the coupons.

A beautiful salsa performance was planned by the hotel staff. The program started with them. The office team performed dances on the retro theme. None of the new hires were part of these programs as they all had recently joined and could not practice. The mahol (ambience) was completely set and everybody was enjoying the appetizers with some drinks. "Ladies and Gentlemen let me reveal that 4 special prizes would be given to the "best dressed female/male/ group and a couple. The judges are amongst you. You might be observed. Be alert and perform well." announced the compère. Everybody started looking around for the judges as no one knew who was adjudicating.

Sneha walked-in with Rimsha. She was wearing a short postal red color dress. It had a deep neck line showing off her cleavage. Big jhumkas which nobody would have thought of wearing with the western styled dress, however, looked pretty on her. She looked taller with those pointed heels. Almost everything she wore was "RED". Her matt red lipstick enticed all the men in room. She looked stunningly hot. Everybody in the room kept looking at her as she looked like a perfect glamour doll.

Amit approached her, "Hey Sneha looking good."

"Really? Thank you so much." replied Sneha. Amit smiled and started looking around just to make sure that he was not making it too palpable for her to realize that he was attracted to her. "What is happening? It is too hot here." said Sneha to Amit. Amit looked at her from top to bottom slanting at her cleavage, "It certainly is. It seems they are going to have some fashion show. They are going to randomly pick up people." Sneha was now a little cautious when the compère called up on her. They also called up Supriya. Supriya definitely had a good dressing sense, and had won all the contests till date. All were asked to do a ramp walk on few numbers. After the fashion show, the compère announced that there were surprise gifts planned for all the winners. Sneha was able to do the cat walk. Sameer too had participated as he was very well dressed in his black shirt with a beige color pant. The compère asked Sameer to be on the stage as he was supposed to make a special announcement.

Sam announced that they had recently formed a BAND called ROCKERS. He introduced all the members in the band and everybody was surprised as no one knew about their talents till then. Sam was the lead guitarist for the band along with two more guys playing guitar, a saxophonist and a drummer. As they were performing, the crowd was clapping and singing with them to encourage them. Rockers were the last to perform for that evening as the compère took over to end the day by calling the winners over. Sneha won the "Lady of the day" and Sameer the "Macho man".

The floor was then open for dance and dj masti (enjoyment). After the floor was open, half of the crowd was near the bar and half on the dance floor. Rest queued for dinner. Everybody was wishing the winners. All the new girls and boys were on stage along with some oldies. They all pulled Amit as well. Amit was dancing with Sneha most of his time. Sneha picked Amit's hands and placed it around her waist. Amit seemed to have been waiting for this moment. "Your skin is really soft." said Amit …while touching Sneha's cheeks. He kept staring at her. While they were getting really close they were being watched by Supriya.

"Would you like to go for a walk on the beach with me asked Sneha?" Sneha seemed very comfortable with Amit. He simply could not deny the proposal. When they were just about to leave the room, Supriya approached them. Supriya went straight to Sneha and slapped her, and shouted "Be in your limits! I have never lost any contest till date and you will repent for this win of yours." This came as shock to everyone including Sneha. She could not believe and did not know how to react. She had never interacted with Supriya except during travel in the train. Supriya was abusing Sneha. Supriya was drunk and had lost it! Rest of the ladies from the mahila mandal group somehow convinced her to stop and move out from there. They had disgusted looks for Sneha. Amit and the HR team had to interfere to ask them leave.

"What happened to her and why me?" asked Sneha to rest of the folks. Everybody commented "ignore her", and "leave it". "This is how Supriya behaves in all the parties. She drinks and abuses whoever she is jealous of. Just because she is quite experienced, we cannot take major steps." said Amit. All of them walked towards the dinner counter. Sneha was trying to figure out the reason for such an outrage.

Sneha remained quiet when Amit said "Let us go for a walk." They both left the dining hall and walked towards the beach. They could hear the waves and moonlight shimmering in the water. The sand was slightly cold and blustery. Amit looked around for some bench to sit. There was none. Amit noticed the parked boat. They walked towards the boat and sat on the same. Amit unpocketed his cigarette pack and started to smoke. Sneha was still down. She kept looking at the waves. "Cheer up!" said Amit. "You have to ignore such people." Sneha looked at him and could not control herself. She hugged him and started crying. Amit a little reluctant though, hugged her back. She was warm and perhaps he wanted to melt in her. Wiping her tears Amit asked her to control herself. With the smoke in his one hand and other tied around Sneha, he could not avoid locking his lips with her. Later Amit could not take his hands off her and they did have an unforgettable time. Suddenly Sneha's phone rang. She shrugged off and started walking away from Amit. "Hi Jaanu (darling), how are you?" asked somebody from the other side. Sneha replied "I am fine, is it OK if I call you back in an hours' time?" And she disconnected. "We need to go back, I am feeling cold and hungry." said Sneha to Amit. They both returned to the dining hall to grab some food.

The funtoosh team members were wrapping up when all heard somebody coughing really loudly, almost as if he was on the verge of puking. Imran puked! This was his first party away from home. He had consumed alcohol for the first time ever. He wanted to taste everything, making it an indigestible cocktail. The funtoosh team was hugely disappointed as the evening was turning into a nightmare now. They closed the bar and dinner counter to avoid any more embarrassments. Sameer and one person from the funtoosh team helped Imran reach his room. They also ensured that he was fine. The funtoosh could not have their dinner and just parted for the day.

Next day was Sunday, last day of the trip. Almost everybody was busy packing and shopping to carry some souvenirs for their dear ones. With some good and few disgusting incidents, the team set for the travel back to Pune. Almost everybody slept while returning. They reached on Monday morning. Rest of the Monday was declared as an OFF.

CHAPTER
Four

"Sometimes my age is very inappropriate for my behavior."

-Anonymous

"Whatever happens in Goa, stays in goa!" However, that statement was less true in this case as everybody who clicked pictures downloaded them to the shared location. The duplication software on the storage was getting tested. About 5 official* (*appointed by the funtoosh team) photographers clicked about 800 photos. They also created so many videos capturing the good, bad and ugly moments including the band performance, Supriya abusing and Imran puking.

Amit did suggest Sneha to forget the incident as Supriya was a part of the same team as Sneha's. And there was no point in taking the matter seriously as Supriya was drunk. However, it was too late for him to suggest anything as Sneha had dropped a complaint email already. Finally Sneha, Supriya, Amit and HR manager decided to meet. "Supriya, you need to apologize to Sneha." said the HR manager. "Why should I, I don't think I need to do that? She is just a new hire and she should mind what she is wearing. Everybody likes what she wears and nobody has problem with her showing the inners. Isn't it? She should apologize in public." said Supriya. Both Amit and the HR manager looked at each other as they were not convinced with the reason Supriya gave for slapping Sneha. The HR manager said, "As long as it fits into the company policy, no one really needs to bother about the same. We don't want to encourage moral policing of any kinds here. We are not in a school to have a monitor explain us the rules. This has happened many times with you Supriya and we have no option but to ask Amit to take strict actions against you." Amit said, "I don't think Sneha should apologize as it is not her mistake. I think it is high time you concentrate on your work assignment. Let us get back to work Supriya." Supriya had more to argue and had no regrets about her behavior. "Amit let us have a one-to-one" said Supriya. One-to-one; a discussion mostly opted to address problems (mostly personal). Amit agreed as he had no other option. "I will see you." said Supriya while gaping at Sneha. Supriya left the room banging the doors. Tears rolled down Sneha's cheeks, as this was her first job and she never expected this to happen in a sophisticated work environment. HR manager requested Amit to leave them alone. "Everybody knows Supriya. She has got bad temperament. She keeps feeling insecure for no reasons." said the HR manager. Besides, Amit had given her lot of authority and attention for no reasons. "Everybody complains about her verbally, nobody has dropped an email except for you. We will definitely take some actions for her. Please wipe off your tears and be bold Sneha, as you will meet such people in any corporate." continued the HR manager. Sneha looked at the HR manager with thousands of questions in her eyes.

Sneha came back to her desk and rushed to washroom. Amit requested Rimsha to check out on her. After 10-15 minutes both of them came back. Upon logging, both of them saw an email from Amit, assigning all of them a task of reading the documents and coming up with a presentation. Sneha was not able to concentrate as she now was looking for evidences to prove things against Supriya. Kavitha, was also going through the documents, taking notes and making presentation herself. Among these three girls, Rimsha, the one who appeared to be dump, completed reading the document before the lunch hours. She kept searching on the web for the content she had to deliver. By EOD (End of day), she sent an email, mentioning she was ready with the presentation on the technology that she was supposed to understand. She had invited everyone to attend the same at around 4.00 PM which is tea-time for most of the folks. However, Amit instructed everybody to be in the room by 4.00. Everybody in the team was speculating about the presentation Rimsha had to make as the task assigned was a little complex. Initially Rimsha was a little nervous, but as she progressed, her confidence was seen. Her first slide said, "Technology is like an ocean and this is my first swimming class, please bear with me till I learn to breathe in water. Please hold on your questions till the end." Her presentation went pretty well. Though it was at very superficial level, she was able to answer the questions. It was evident that Amit was very impressed by Rimsha and was spellbound. After Rimsha's presentation, he wrote an email, congratulating Rimsha for delivering the presentation and asking others older than her to learn from her. Even if it was downloaded from the web, everybody wanted to pat Rimsha on her back as it does take lots of guts to read through a presentation on the first assignment itself. Rimsha now became Amit's favorite# 3 as Sneha was always his first choice in recent times.

"Let us go for a chai (tea)." requested Amit to Sneha after Rimsha finished her presentation. Sneha agreed and everybody saw something that had never happened. Amit would never go for chai or dinner with his team members. He would always go with his equivalent in hierarchy. That was for the first time. First time he was extending his work hours. He normally would leave office by 5.00 PM and re-login from home. Amit who never shared any knowledge with anybody unless asked, would give Sneha all the TOIs* (*Transfer of Information). Apparently, he had asked HR to leave a cube empty next to him. Even if a manager wants to have 100% transparency, he has to maintain some level of confidentiality. Sneha was asked to move in that empty cube and she did not mind that.

Amit started arranging all sort of KTs* (*Knowledge

transfers) for her. He had convinced the technically expert members to mentor Sneha. Sneha would accompany Amit everywhere and vice versa except some obvious places. He used to explain her each and every component in great details. To make Sneha visible amongst the executives, Amit would invite Sneha for meetings which she was not required to attend. Amit would create presentations for Sneha and Sneha would also read through them.

Empathy, sympathy or something else? Everybody was trying to guess as to what was going on. On the other hand, Supriya was going through tough times. Amit along with HR had given Supriya warning to change her behavior or else she would have to resign. She could not believe that Amit was doing that to her as she was one of his favorites at some point in time. She felt disgraced and requested the HR manager to change her team. Changing the team would change her reporting manager; however, no manager was eager to hire Supriya. Supriya did escalate the matter to all the executives she knew, but nobody was willing to help her. She had no option but to stay in Amit's team. It seemed that one of the senior executives whom Supriya trusted a lot advised her not to leave the job or Amit's team as "Changing manager or team is not the solution for problems, it might create more problems. Whatever happens face them". With lot of revenge on her mind she thought of trying it out.

Time was taking revenge for Sneha. She was seeing Supriya loose. She was excited and very happy. She used this opportunity as much as she could and got very close to Amit. This in turn caused a lot of lag in terms of work. She would do anything that Amit wanted her to. For example, get the printout from the printer. Create some setups* (* which She never created) which he would then assign to other team members for work.

She always took help from the Lab team. Most of organizations have a separate IT support or the lab teams. Most of them being men, exceptions are there. These are the super helpful folks. They technically have superb knowledge of installing, configuring and maintaining the equipment required for developing and testing the final products. They also take care of maintaining all the domain controllers and connectivity issues between various sites. They are the most hardworking people and most sweet spoken people too. And people who would also know lot of inside news too :-)

Whenever there was a setup to be created, Sneha would file a ticket instead of creating it herself. She would go in the cabin where all the Lab team would sit and start with "Good morning guys, I need some help." All the overworked admins would turn around replying, "Hey Sneha, please have a seat. How can we help you? Would you like to have some tea/coffee?" They would then ask the office boys (who would smile, as that was a special treatment) to get masala tea for "Sneha madam". "Oh I just had tea with Amit. Can somebody help me with a setup creation? That OS installation is not working with the images I have and also the cable connection would require somebody tall like you to help me with." The team would have a look at the ticket filed by Sneha immediately while she was around and commit that they will complete it by EOD. Sneha would then sit there and have tea while talking over few other things. "I saw your latest picture on Facebook, very nice picture and you look so good." said one of the lab admins to Sneha. Sneha replied "Is it? One of my friends casually clicked it when we had gone to Mahableshwar. I did read your comment "You look awesome" and replied to it too." Sneha had about 1000 friends on Facebook. She would post 4 times a day and every picture she posted got several 100s of likes and comments. Since the time she had joined, most of the men had added her in their friend list and she had accepted them too. "What else is happening with you guys." asked Sneha. "Nothing madam, just going on. We will drop you an email once the work is done." replied one of the admins.

After that Sneha would go with her laptop to the lab. IT labs are very sophisticated and cold places. It is a place where most of the equipment is placed and then it is connected to the outer network for accessibility. She would stay in the lab, doing some work till the time she got a reply from the lab team. Generally the lab team won't wait for EOD (End of Day) to complete the task. They would do it immediately for her. Sneha would then inform Amit that she completed the setup. Amit would then send an email appreciating her. Sneha was performing more like an assistant than an Engineer. Every day the team members felt as if they were watching some Bollywood movie 'boss-secretary' scene. The way she spoke with the boss, she never spoke the same tender way with anybody else. She used all her skills to lure him... People normally used the Gtalk or Yahoo messenger to ask for something. Everybody in the team used to think, as to what was wrong with Amit as he seemed to be very witty before Sneha came in. He was quite neutral to everybody. No doubt, he was very chatty and did like talking with everybody. He was a known flamboyant. In fact, he was rated as one of the best manager in the organization. He was in love with her. What kind of love, was not known to anybody.

Amit asked the HR to modify the policy to make Sneha permanent in 3 months rather than 6 months. **She was exceeding the expectation. She was now a *Performer**. HR team resisted but he used his power to bypass. Everybody on the floor was surprised as everybody knew that she was technically just fine as compared to her other batch mates. People reported to have seen both Amit and Sneha in malls, theatres and restaurants together. They were spending a lot of time together. Amit was spending lot of his money too. On asking what was going on, they would reply "We are good friends." Friendship between a "senior manager" and a "new hire" had become the talk of town. In another 3 months, Sneha was promoted as the Senior Software Engineer. Fastest promotion!

CHAPTER
Five

"There is something wrong in your character,
if opportunity controls your loyalty."

-Anonymous

"Sweets at my desk, got engaged (EOM)." Everybody saw an email from Sneha. It was a little shocking for those who did not know that Sneha was committed to a childhood friend and was dating him for years. So! But! And! Everybody in the office had many such questions in their mind and "chai pe charcha" (talk over tea) sessions. Everyone congratulated her and immediately referred to Facebook to find out who the Prince charming was or who the UN/lucky person was! This email from Sneha had created a big turbulence, as she had broken heart/s. Sneha was happy and blushing while everybody congratulated her. Obviously, she had got everything in last one year which everybody dreamt of; Permanent Job, Promotion and marriage. She was on cloud nine.

"You are looking gorgeous today." said Sameer. Sneha blushed! She replied, "Of course, I must be! I had been to parlor yesterday." Sameer as usual replied "So was the parlor closed"? He thought of pulling her leg when both he and Imran had dropped in her cube to get some sweets for themselves. "What do you mean? I look beautiful naturally?" asked Sneha. "I spent 6000/- yesterday." Imran was, like, "That's it?" and looked at Sameer. Sameer further asked her which parlor and what all she did, which she refused to reply.

"Congrats – Amit (Please excuse typos, sent from an iPhone)." replied Amit to her engagement-announcing email. He had some personal issues to address at home which is why he was late to office on that day. As soon as Amit came to office, he called Sneha for a 1-1. It went on for an hour. Everybody in the team was roaming around the meeting room to get the glance of whatever was happening inside. But all the meeting rooms are sound proof. So even if somebody shouts on top of their voice, nobody would know. Besides, the glasses are perforated, so one cannot see too. One question that everybody in the team had

"What's happening inside?"

Amit: Congratulations! (He hugged her.) You never told me about you being in relation.

Sneha: You never asked.

Amit: C'mon you tell me everything. Why not this?

This time Amit had 100s of questions in his eyes.

Sneha: I was not too sure about getting engaged to him.

Amit: So what about our relation?

Sneha: Which relation Amit? You are my manger and I work for you. Apart from this, we are friends.

Amit: Just friends!

Sneha: Okie, friends with some benefits.

Amit: Friends with benefits? Who is benefitting out of this relation Sneha you or me? What about the time we spent in Goa?

Sneha: Goa? What in Goa? Oh. C'mon we are grown up adults and at times we have to give it all for our physical desires. Which I did and you too. That was the need of that time.

Amit: It would be just a physical need for you, but I love you Sneha. (He shrugged her.)

Sneha: You loved Supriya too? Didn't you?

Amit: Are you crazy?

Sneha: Amit you are being childish and possessive. That was just a night stand. You are married and having two daughters. I am quite sure you won't leave them for me. Is it not true?

Amit: "Ah... Oh no. not like that. But I still love you."

Sneha: I respect that, and we shall continue being

friends. Everything is going on well and I really want to flourish in my career. You are my best mentor.

Amit: You used me. I promoted you by going against the rules and you are saying; let us remain friends.

Sneha: I thought you promoted me for my work.

Amit: Your work. Are you crazy? What work you did? What excellence you achieved? I regret promoting you.

Sneha: You used me too Amit. To satisfy your mid-life crisis. If you think that I never understood that, then that is incorrect. Amit, I shall still give you what you need..

Amit slapped Sneha saying she was a Gold-digger and she had hurt him. On this Sneha replied, "I know what you are Amit. And I will make sure that you repent for this. I am not Supriya. BTW, you cannot hurt somebody whom you don't love." And she left the room. Sneha did not have many friends in office, hence the chances of discussion getting leaked was minimum. It seemed Sneha never told about her relationship to anybody, it was very personal. Not even to Amit, who spent so much time with her. As a friend Amit might have expected that from her. Amit came out of the room quite casually. "Leaving early, not feeling well." Both Amit and Sneha left for the day. Amit was hurt and it was evident from his behavior.

This incident had to have repercussions. Amit assigned her task more than what he did earlier. He made sure that she had to wait longer than normal working hours. Sneha knew very little about the organization's product, forget product, she knew less about the feature she tested. She kept making test-beds for the other teammates. So what would she do to complete her task? To get the things done, Sneha was now getting closer to another person in team. She started taking help from him. All men in the team were eager to help her and so was the new friend of hers. Story was repeating, hero had changed and expectations too. She avoided Amit. She denied all his lunch, tea and snack invites. She now started going with her new friend. This person was smart though and knew the background. Extremely shrewd and cunning in nature. He was married too and had a kid. So what…? Friend is a friend. But for Sneha, he was something more than a friend.

Amit knew him very well and was being protective for Sneha. He warned Sneha against him. But she was in no mood to listen as she was now a rebellion. Noticing that Amit was jealous, she started going more close to the other guy. Amit always was a Villain for many others, but for Sneha he had transformed from friend to a Villain. Sneha's new friend could complete all the work for her and rescue her from the assigned task. Later in the evening, they would go for drives on his bike. People could see them in malls, theatres and restos around on weekends. Even if she was completing her work, as an **expectation from Senior Engineer she was not performing**. Amit did not sit quiet and he pulled her on **PIP (Performance improvement plan)**. Now this is a time, when the employer gives a last chance to the employee to prove him/herself if they are performing really bad. Sneha was not the person who would sit quite. She filed a case against Amit about abusing her sexually and mentally torturing her. In order to prove her own self, she formed a union with 3-4 guys to trouble him. She kept accusing Amit. Everybody in the organization started noticing the *performer in her diminishing phase.

The HR ignored her emails and did not bother to reply her as Amit was close to the HR. The HR did warn Amit about the happenings. Everybody in the organization was shocked to have seen something like this. Since Sneha did not get reply from the HR team, she escalated the matter to the legal team who takes care of harassment cases. The HR who received the complaint and who did not take action was fired. Amit had to go through a lot of interrogations by the internal committees. He was in the industry for a longer time and had all data points to prove himself correct. Sneha was not able to prove her side as the favors she got from Amit were questioned. Why did Amit promote you? Amit was asked the same question, but he had data to prove his act. All the registers, all the meeting requests and all the emails were sniffed. Her nature of asking help in return of something in favor was highlighted. What favors, not known to anyone. She had lost it. She was asked to resign. Amit was asked to take a sabbatical for 6 months. Sneha lost her job.

Amit had a very strong network and almost everybody in his network had strong hold in various organizations. He made sure nobody hired her. She applied to a lot of other domains post that event. But nobody hired her, as most of the organizations have serious verification procedure. She got married with the person she was engaged to. After their marriage, they left for Australia and she settled down with him. Sneha's friend was asked to resign as he was part of conspiracy too. Lot of "messenger chats" of his with Sneha against Amit were found. He was able to get a job at a different location, but not in the same city.

CHAPTER
Six

*"Friend in need (of a job), may not be
a friend IN-DEED."*

-Anonymous

After Sneha's exit, and after treading through all the interrogations that happened, Amit would often be lost in his own world. He was not able to focus on his work. Yet he would stay late in office and avoid home as well. Certainly, few things reflected back at home too. On a rainy Friday evening, while sitting in his cube, he was looking at his Facebook account. He saw a post by his friend Pankaj "Proud to be a recipient of the President's Award". "What the f$$$? How the hell he would get this award? He seems to be really lucky to have received this? Otherwise he was just a normal person." said Amit to himself. Feeling restless, Amit walked towards the smoking zone. While smoking, he just went back in time. Almost 15 years back. In his very first job. He started recollecting the hard time his boss gave him in the last organization he worked for. The last encounter with his boss was what made him run for cover and that was how he was reintroduced to Pankaj.

Boss: Did you achieve your allocated target Amit?

Amit: (Hesitantly) No sir.

Boss: What the FXXX you do all day around? Not even a single customer you could get in this month! Ridiculous.

Fetching his Classic-Milds from his left-pocket, he gave Amit disgusting looks.

Boss: This is the last warning "you better perform" or...

Amit speechless

Boss: Leave now.

Amit was very stressed when he left the boss's cabin. His desk was at the extreme corner of the office. While walking through the passage, he had many thoughts in his mind. He remembered the times, when he was awarded the "Best employee". He had pretty good relation with his ex-manager. His ex-manager was asked to leave for faking results and the organization had hired another person. This new boss of Amit, was unhappy with him since day one.

"I am a MBA, he cannot talk like this to me." said Amit to himself while settling in the chair. He was with the organization for 2 years now. He was fed-up with the work, the new boss and the remuneration he got. He was looking for an opportunity in cities like Pune, Mumbai or Bangalore. With all the thoughts in mind, Amit logged on to Facebook. While browsing through Facebook, he saw his friend Pankaj's update about some requirements in his organization. Amit picked his phone and called up his friend Pankaj.

Amit: Hi Pankaj, how are you dear?

Pankaj: Hey Amit, long time. I am fine, how about you?

Amit: Hey listen (walking towards a conference room), I am in trouble. I need your help. I need a job.

Pankaj: Sure. But we do not have any requirements in Marketing.

Amit: I am OK with moving into Engineering. Can you please help?

Pankaj: Sure thing Amit, I will try my best. Send me your resume.

Amit: Do I have to modify for engineering role?

Pankaj: No, that is not required.

Amit: Thank you so much dear. Please get me out from this.

Pankaj: Sure. Bye

Pankaj and Amit were in same school. Amit would always ask for help and Pankaj would always help him. Amit never enquired about Pankaj unless he needed some help. Pankaj selected to study engineering and Amit opted for Business administration. They were not in touch with each other for long years. Later on, Amit got to know that Pankaj was placed in a multinational company and earned much more than Amit. As soon as he knew that, he got in touch with friends who knew Pankaj and collected his credentials.

Pankaj did not change, he was hardworking, modest and helping others was his topmost desire. "Pankaj, there is one task which nobody in the team wants to do as that is not the trending technology and it will be obsolete soon. Would you like to take up that task?" Pankaj would not think for a single moment, and agree to do it. Pankaj was known for his flexible and sharing nature. One of his fortes was creating very useful documents. He would be interacting with customer and the project manager directly. He never underestimated any work, any technology or judged the task. He did what was required and what he thought should be done the best.

He got many awards and recognitions not just from the top management but his peers too. **He was a STAR (not *) Performer, as he genuinely worked more than expected. He was exceeding the expectations.** Even if he could not help, he knew who would help. Apart from being a good co-worker, Pankaj had deep interest in social activities and would participate in all CSR activities (Corporate Social Responsibilities). He had taken initiatives to plant trees in areas around office. When Pankaj had joined, the organization was small. It had 50 odd people. When higher management thought of expanding the workforce, Pankaj was a part of the hiring team and was also referring people he knew. He would help them on how should they prepare for interviews and he also followed up with the Talent Acquisitions teams for the feedback and communicated back to them. He was very helpful and that's what made him help Amit too.

"Good morning, Pankaj. How are you? Listen, I have my first round tomorrow. Can you tell me, what questions they would ask?" inquired Amit. "Hi, I am fine Amit. I would suggest you to be yourself and prepare on whatever is mentioned in the resume." replied Pankaj.

"Is there anything else that they would ask?" checked Amit. "Well I cannot share much details, as I do not know who is taking the interview. But just be confident." was Pankaj's reply. "Sure Bro" and he still insisted on asking more question. Whenever Amit was called by the interviewer, he would give an excuse and postpone the interview. As Amit was Pankaj's referral, he was given time. Amit Googled more on the answers provided by Pankaj and prepared himself. He kept calling Pankaj, and kept clearing all the rounds. After Amit's face-to-face interview, the manager commented that he was not the right fit and that he should be kept on hold. Pankaj had very less say in that comment, but he said that he will help Amit learn the technology. He would make sure that Amit ramped up in no time. The hiring Manager was assured and he thought of offering Amit. This was how Amit got his job in the same organization. Pankaj did not mention about that favour to Amit as he was modest enough to not show off. Had it been anybody else, he surely would have done the "power demonstration".

Pankaj, believed in providing opportunities to people. He himself had struggled all his life and felt grateful to God for whatever he had. Pankaj came from a place, which in spite of being part of a city like Mumbai, had no TOILETS. He lived in a Mumbai chawl. His dad expired when he was just 9 year old and his mom raised him by running "tea+ kande pohe (an Indian snack) stall". He could complete his education as some people donated their books, and sponsored his education. Amit knew a little about this.

Amit joined the company. From day one Amit was with Pankaj. He wanted to learn everything. Everything that Pankaj learned in so many years, in just few days. Pankaj too proactively explained Amit everything in details. He shared all the documents he had prepared without having a second thought. Amit kept on asking questions and Pankaj kept answering. Amit was initially working in another team, and not Pankaj's team. But it was for the same product. Due to some reorganization, Pankaj had to join Amit's team. This team was now led by a manager who was new too. As soon as Pankaj joined Amit's team, Amit felt insecure. This made him compete against Pankaj rather than working with him or giving him credit for the help he offered. Amit started backbiting about Pankaj everywhere he went.

Pankaj ignored and kept on doing the work, the way he did earlier. He would never worry about Amit's behaviour. Apart from working in IT, Pankaj was running his own foundation. It was a registered foundation. It was not an NGO, but his own company. He always dreamt of doing something for the people. He had a lot of affection for women as he had seen his mother struggle. In every woman, he could see his mom. "Matra dev bhava" was the tagline for the foundation he ran. Pankaj's dream was to build toilets which were clean, hygienic and affordable for every woman who worked for her own survival.

As per Amit, Pankaj was the person born with a silver spoon who would work less and spend more time in activities not related to office. Amit was presenting himself as a person who had done all the research, who had taken all the efforts and who deserved a promotion. Pankaj was noticing this. "You do good and good will return to you." was Pankaj's funda of life. That was why he kept on doing what he was. Amit in fact, fought for promotion and he got it too. In spite of being at higher designation than Pankaj, team members would still ask Pankaj for help. That was hurting Amit. He did not like people praising Pankaj. Amit influenced their manager to write an email to everybody saying that "any questions related to this particular feature should be pointed to Amit and nobody else". The only work that Amit now was doing was finding mistakes in Pankaj's work. He now wanted to present himself as a person who would run behind Pankaj to get the work done. He nagged him.

Pankaj was very neutral to all that Amit was doing and waiting for his NGO to be funded. One day everybody in the team got the email from Pankaj saying "Today is my last day in the organization." Pankaj was very happy, and shared some of the last moments with his friends there. Amit joined the conversation and said "You never told me man." Pankaj remained silent for a moment and replied "Now you know it." Amit had nothing to say as he was the second happiest person in the world after Pankaj's exit. The competition which he had started, Pankaj left it half-way.

Though Pankaj had left the organization, Amit was still following Pankaj on his social network. After few months, he had realized that Pankaj had opted to be a social entrepreneur and was in news most of the time. Pankaj never forgot what Amit did to him as well. However, he did not break any relation with Amit and continued to be friends with him.

When Amit realized that Pankaj was working on providing toilets to less fortunate, he made fun of him. "Silly Pankaj! Left such glamorous and high paying job for such a stupid thing." thought Amit when he read Pankaj's post. Amit simply felt jealous and that made him restless yet again. With that restlessness, Amit shutdown his laptop and walked towards his peer Rohan for a tea-break or to vent out his frustration. "Rohan, how about some tea?"

CHAPTER
Seven

"Good things happen to those,
who ~~wait~~ / know how to get the SHIT DONE."

-Anonymous

After returning from US, he always ran behind showing himself different. He kept on comparing the working styles of the US teams with Indian teams. **"This is not how it works there"** was what he claimed time and again. He carried that typical American accent which everybody else would make fun of in his absence. "Walk the talk", "don't work like donkeys, use your brains", "IMHO" and "AFAIK" were his most commonly used phrases.

Rohan was in United States for almost 20 years and had returned to India for family reasons. He was super smart. Very intelligent and technically profound. Nobody could make a fool out of him. He had a good track record of being different. As soon as he joined the Pune office, he started an initiative called "USE LESS ENERGY". This initiative was started to save the electricity. Electricity used by the equipment in the labs, or electricity used by the central air conditioner or the desktops. Electricity is very expensive in India as compared to the other locations. Hence, to save the Earth from global warming, many organizations run the "USE LESS ENERGY" activities. It was a good initiative and it definitely saved a lot of money for the organization as well it saved the electricity especially when we all know the importance Power and the amount of load shedding that happens in our state. There are so many villages which do not have electricity yet and people have to depend on other resources for lighting their houses. Every Friday, Rohan would host a meeting for "USE LESS ENERGY" efforts. Some people were inspired by him and had volunteered to be part of the effort. But soon they realized that the initiative was to just to prove him different. He was not much concerned about saving electricity as he never turned off his monitor while leaving. He had put up screen savers made from his pictures clicked while receiving awards. That was not "WALK THE TALK".

In most of the organizations, there are at least 2-3 huge printers setup per floor for the employees to print. It can be for their personal or professional use. There are no restrictions as such. It is just to make the employee's life easy. So that they can focus more on work and facilities can offload such tasks from them. One day around 2.00 PM to 2.30 PM, when everybody on the floor was busy working, they heard the printer making a screeching noise. Generally, people would take 2-3 printouts or at the max 10. But the printer was not stopping; somebody had printed a story book of 300 pages. That printing went on for 15 minutes. Every printout would have the name of the person who issued the printouts and some would configure it to be password protected. Everybody had gathered near the printer to find out who issued that printing. That particular printing job was issued by Rohan and he was embarrassed as he saw everybody around the printer. "Oh ho... by mistake I clicked on the print button." He justified. That was something against "Please don't make use of printers for personal use." stated by him. That was not "GOING GREEN" or "SAVING PAPER".

So many times, he took printouts of cartoon characters and home work sheets for his daughters. He had two daughters but he never got them to office on any of the "KID'S DAY". His team members knew as the driver who dropped them to school in the office car told them. Yes, he had opted for the "chauffer driven car". His designation allowed him to do so.

Rohan was very concerned about his designation and showed it off wherever and whenever possible. He carried his designation everywhere. "I am a Manager. 18-20 people report to me. I get the work done from them." said Rohan to every person he met. He always showed off as if the organization was running because of him. "Well, I cannot take leaves. As it will be a huge loss to the organization." Lot of people referred to an incident that became very famous. It seemed on one weekend, Rohan with his wife and daughters had been to super market. He was done shopping and was waiting in a long queue for paying the bills. It was a busy Saturday evening and the super market was crowded. There were at least 6-7 people in front of him. He was getting restless. He somehow managed to trespass to person who was at billing counter. "How long would you take for such a small work? You all are the same. Open big markets and not able to handle the same. Useless, do you know who I am?" The boy at the billing counter was cool and replied "No sir, how would I know. Also, whoever you are please be in line and do not disturb me as it will delay the work further. Please wait in queue for your turn."

On this Rohan said "I was in the US for years and have returned here. So many educated people report to me. Unlike you. You must be just a 10th grade pass." He seized the collar and asked him for his supervisor." The boy at billing counter ignored him and pointed Rohan to his supervisor. The answer supervisor gave, shattered him. "Sir, you work for such a reputed company. Why you want to talk to small people like us? This is how we work. In case you are in hurry, feel free to visit another mart."

Rohan was furious and in all his frustration he said "You will regret what you said. I will give extremely bad review about you people." The supervisor gave him his business card and left from the place. Rohan's wife tried a lot to stop him, but she could not. She was embarrassed. Rohan left without the stuff. Almost 2 trolleys full of groceries.

Rohan, 5 feet 6 inches tall. Straight nose and slightly fair. He was well built and well groomed. Bad tempered and low tolerance levels. He always overcommitted. He used to put the team in pressure and make them work for the date he mentioned just to save his skin. In every status meeting, he would accuse the person for the work they did and why they were not able to complete it on time. According to him, coding a feature, or fixing a bug should not take more than 4 hours. Testing that fix should not take more than an hour.

He made sure that he was a part of everything like fun committees, sports committees or CSR committees. Initially he did not have much say, later on things were happening as he said. Of course that required lot of credibility to be established and he had achieved that. Most of the IT organizations have quarterly and yearly parties besides every release party. Release party happens when a particular feature is delivered/released to customer/s. All the expenses were bared by the organization. This as per Rohan was "WASTE". He thought that there was nothing good about those parties at exotic location and nobody was really participating. Besides, the organization was investing too much which it should not. He started arranging parties in office. Something likes a samosa party or bhel (Indian savoury snack) party. He conveyed that to the top management as most liked events and he also showcased that he saved a lot of dollars. That made him visible and gained him more credit.

People started realizing his hypocrisy when he took the credit on saving the money from the employee engagement activities. Whenever he had his boss visiting, he made sure he took him to the coolest place to eat and stay, making sure that he left with a good impression of his own self. "People in my team are very happy. They were bored with the earlier celebrations." commented Rohan. He stopped everything that would make a team member happy. Be it a promotion, be it a celebration or travel. In case he knew any travel opportunities coming, he would grab that for his own self. Thus, not allowing any member to travel and even if they did, he made sure that the arrangements made were cheaper so that no one would ever ask for it again. Nobody in Rohan's team was growing. He never recommended anyone for any promotion, or rewards. Because all efforts that team made were his and he could convince that on the top. With lot of initiatives and cheaper money saving strategies, Rohan fought for the Promotion, as per him he was "Exceeding expectation. He was promoted".

CHAPTER
Eight

"If you are not a supporter of the chief, you're an outcast.
IF you are a supporter of the chief, you're in.
Favoritism, it is!"

"**H**e is self-obsessed. Cannot think beyond himself. Me, me and me. Has he ever promoted anybody? He portrays as if he is the only one working and we all do nothing." said Neetu to another female colleague who was in listening mode only. "Of course, it requires lot of skill and Rohan is very good at it. He gets everything done from us and is still able to fake. No wonder he is at that position." said Neetu. The colleague replied "True yaar (dear)." "Anyway I have to take an interview of a very seasoned and experienced person. Almost double of my experience." said Neetu. "How are you going to manage?" asked the female colleague. "I have Kunal with me. You know how he is! He will simply reject this candidate you see." replied Neetu. Adding to that she said "Kunal himself is so arrogant that if someone in an interview does not answer in Kunal's format, then he straight away rejects him. He will manage it. See you in an hour's time." Neetu then rushed to the conference room which was next to her cubicle. The candidate was already in and waiting for the interviewers.

Neetu: Hi, My name is Neeta and I will be accompanied by my colleague Kunal for this round. Let us wait for him.

Candidate: Sure Neeta.

Neetu: you can call me Neetu, that's how everyone addresses me. She smiled.

Candidate: Sure, Neetu.

Neetu: Would you like to have anything? The coffee that our vending machine makes is awesome. You should try it.

Candidate: Which vending machine it is?

Neetu: Not sure, I will have to check.

Candidate: I am good, thank you.

Meanwhile the candidate was looking at his watch, as the interview was supposed to start 15 minutes back.

Kunal entered the room with a coffee mug in his hand.

Kunal: Hey sorry bro (brother), I was in mid of something, had to keep you waiting.

Candidate: No problem.

Kunal: Can you please brief about you, may be in 2 minutes as I need to rush in other meeting?

Candidate: Certainly, but briefing about vast experience in just 2 minutes is challenging.

Kunal: For how long have you been working in IT?

Candidate: 18 years (quite casually).

Kunal: That's pretty long.

Candidate: May be

Neetu: Just some highlights of your career will help us.

The candidate shared his career highlights and the technology he worked on. Based on that Kunal had another question,

Kunal: My next question should be easy for you...

"How do you ensure quality of your product" in one sentence please?

Candidate: Code coverage is one of the widely used tool.

Both Neetu and Kunal looked at each other as they were not happy with the answer he gave.

Kunal: Ok, we are done with the questions. The hiring team should get back to you.

Neetu: Thank you.

Candidate: Thank you.

Neetu and Kunal walked out of the conference room. While walking towards their cubicles, Kunal was still sipping his coffee.

Neetu: Did you find him arrogant?

Kunal: Yes and I am going to write the same in feedback form.

Neetu: What is code coverage?

Kunal: What Neetu? Don't you know it? I think it is a tool which these QA folks use. You should be knowing it better as you are from QA and have spent more time in company than me.

Neetu: Shut up you fighter cock. We don't use the same here. Number of PASS and FAIL cases are good enough for our executives to understand the quality of product.

Kunal: I should have taken your interview, I would have never hired you Neetu.

Neetu: Thank God! Otherwise we would have never had anybody in the organization. Just you and Rohan (giggled).

Kunal: Please send the feedback form.

Neetu: You send it yourself; I am not doing it for you this time.

Kunal: Okay!

Neetu and Kunal; Rohan's right and left arm. Whenever he said, "I literally know who thinks what about me." everybody knew how. Yes, they were his "Karan-Arjun". Karan and Arjun, the "Mere do anmol ratan" which every manager has. Well they can be anyone, difficult to spot them but with experience one should be able to figure that out. Kunal had almost 9 years of experience in IT industry. And comparatively more favourite than Neetu.

When Kunal joined the organization, he felt that he was offered a title less than he deserved and the salary was way to less than those on board already. In his previous organization he had several patents filed which was the reason behind his popularity amongst executives. He was technically sound and was good at whatever he did. He helped Rohan with all his technical decision making, be it interviews, or planning or operations handling. As Rohan had worked more with the US teams, his experience with Indian teams was less, Kunal would help Rohan with that.

Kunal, a chain smoker, he smoked more than he breathed. He was flabby and arrogant. Once a team member from another team approached him for some technical queries. The person who approached was more experienced than him and was with the organization for longer time, but he did not have much exposure to the technical aspect of the project which both of them were supposed to work on. He asked Kunal to help him. Kunal who always made everybody feel that he was the most worked out person, replied to him very arrogantly saying "Man you are way experienced than me, how come you don't know this." He said this very loudly and the senior person was embarrassed. On top of that, Kunal said "I am too busy. Please drop an email to me and copy Rohan on that. I shall get back to you when I have time."

The duo would always be on cloud 9 as they were blessed by the boss. They were blessed as they felt they were the "bestest". Yea, this was the title given to them. Kunal and Neetu were a part of the interview panel too and Rohan relied hell lot on their comments for the decision to hire. For the sake of process, Rohan would involve other team members who were equally capable but their comments did not matter. The objective they had while taking interviews was "to prove the person down, rather than hiring him/her". They would confuse a person so that he panicked and was not able to confidently answer or lose interest in giving the interview. Those who were smart could pass them, but not everyone. Their interview feedbacks were Juvenile. Something like, "he/she does not deserve that title/salary". Everything for them was mapped in terms of "number of years of experience". If a person has so much experience, then he/she should know it all. Comparison with their own self. "If I know this, if I have gone out of the way to understand something then every person on other side should have done that." Neetu, was technically average. She was a part of all the events and non-work related activities. "I agree to disagree" would be her concluding statement. In all the meetings, she would argue with Rohan. It would appear as if they were fighting. She would complain about him to every person so much that a person would be empathic to her and join her in complaining. She would then go and tell to Rohan ☺. It obviously had repercussions. She would update

Rohan about what was going on and what was trending in the organization. It would help Rohan whenever he had to speak about it. Initially, very few knew about that but later on it was known to everyone, which was why nobody trusted her.

They had complaints for every process, every other person, and anyone. They could do this because they knew they were heard. For rest of the team, all the feedbacks were ignored. The trio was responsible for a very sincere, technically profound and 'immensely popular amongst the colleagues' kind of a person to be terminated. He had same number of experience as of Rohan. He preferred to remain a technical person rather than getting into the management path. Most of the plans suggested by Rohan were prepared by Kunal and at times he was not able to convince about the same, Kunal would chip in. Somehow or because of the experience level he had, he realized that the plan was incomplete or will not work. On that Kunal would challenge him and Rohan would support him. They pressurized the person and Rohan asked him to resign.

"Kunal, can you buddy Sameer?" Rohan had asked Kunal when Sameer joined. Kunal as usual "Rohan, I am really overworked. I have to do this and that. Also, is Sameer from Sneha's batch? Can you please ask Praveen to do the same? Besides, why would he need a buddy? He is an IIT pass out and most of the time he is in the smoking zone with his guitar. I don't want to mentor such a person." Kunal was a human camera installed by Rohan for monitoring who was working and who was smoking. The real reason for Kunal to deny Rohan's request was he knew that even though Sameer had joined as a fresher, he was far more intelligent than Kunal and was a fast learner. Ask Sameer anything and he had an answer. Being just a software engineer, he was well versed with the product Architecture and the entire stack. At times, when Sameer used to ask for information, Kunal would deny with the fear of losing his knowledge to him.

The only problem with Sam was, he never did anything more than he was asked to. He had deep interest in music and was very passionate about the same. Sameer was part of a renowned band who would do major events around the country. Sameer was a social media addict and had a lot of fan following. The reason he was working was he was equally passionate about technology. He did not care much about the ratings and the money offered as he was more content with happiness he got by playing guitar. Rohan knew Sam's capabilities yet was less insecure. Rohan asked Praveen to mentor Sameer and he agreed. Sameer was very happy as he too wanted to be with Praveen. Praveen being the coolest, and helpful. Everybody had very high regards for him and so did Sam. Sameer was made permanent, but not promoted in spite of the fact that he was far better than Sneha. In fact, when Sameer asked for the promotion, he was told by Amit that the fresher's are not promoted unless they complete 2 years with the organization. Sameer asked something which he should not have had "Why was Sneha promoted twice within a year?". "Some exceptions are there" replied Amit. Pat came the reply from Sameer "And who decides the exceptions?" Amit replied in anger "You shall understand soon." and moved Sameer to Rohan's team.

CHAPTER

"Criticism comes to those who STAND OUT."

-Seth Godin

After moving from Amit's team, Sameer had to change his workstation and shift to the place closer to Rohan's team. The cube had his Guitar stand around, posters of his favourite artists, and quite a few pictures from his own concerts. Few of them were with celebrities. Some small indoor plants and a basketball ring on one of the walls. He was still unpacking, when he saw a frame which read the quote below. He thought of mounting the same and was doing so when he heard someone giggle. "What is funny?" asked Sam

---

Everybody thinks if you do one thing,
you can't do something else.

So I like the fact that I can be versatile if I want to.

-Denise Van Outen"

Neetu who had the habit of peeping in other's workplaces said, "We all understand Sam what you want to say." She giggled more and left from there. When Sam was about to say something, he got a message on his screen "Ignore her", wrote Praveen to Sam. Sameer replied "Why", on that Praveen wrote

"You don't need to respond to every comment, avoiding interrupts hog your CPU less". Both of them had a hearty laugh. Sameer asked Praveen for tea on the messenger and Praveen agreed.

Sameer used to sit right next to Praveen and he used to observe Praveen a lot. The way he worked, spoke with team mates and how curious he would be to learn something new. Praveen never smoked, yet he accompanied Sameer every time he went unless Sameer was escorted by somebody from the funtoosh team. "Why should I ignore her?" asked Sameer to Praveen when they were walking towards the "chai tapri". "CHAI TAPRI", generally a tea stall, but mostly a place to gossip about boss and team members not present there at that point of time. Since the boom of IT industry, the chai tapris and the income of people who run chai tapris have grown enormously. No matter how fancy and comfortable pantries are made, people prefer to go to the "chai tapri". This is the place where most of the plans and strategies are developed. Innovations are thought of and all the frustrations are vented out; also a place where singles come out looking for eligible options. Best place to network as people from various companies around come to this place. The best thing is the "chai wala anna" (tea seller) would know who would be the next person to go Onsite, or who would resign and where is he going. Which company is hiring and who is the next CEO☺.

"Why did you stop me from responding to Neetu, asked Sameer to Praveen"? Praveen looked around and said to Sam, "Neetu was Rohan's Karan-Arjun." "Really, but they fight a lot." said Sameer. "Yes that is what she showcases. But the truth is she is an informer. She would be very sweet on face, but once the person leaves, she would complain and curse the person. "Interesting" replied Sameer.

Praveen suggested Sam to complete all his work on time and also apply for an internal talent hunt. Sameer disclosed to Praveen that he was thinking of a complete change in career. Sameer was going through a selection procedure for another ESTABLISHED band as a lead guitarist. Being in this band would get him the opportunity to perform internationally with renowned artists. On this Praveen just patted him on the back and opened his hand asking for an autograph. "I am honoured to be sitting with you and enjoying the tea dear." said Praveen to Sam. Sam was overwhelmed and both of them happily came back to their desk. While walking Sam told Praveen not to disclose it anyone. Praveen was the man of his words. He assured Sam to trust him.

After they came from the chai tapri, Kunal asked

Praveen and Sam if they were interested in having tea. They replied saying they just had one at the tapri. Kunal asked Rohan and they both went for tea at the same "Chai tapri". Apparently, Kunal was very good at getting information. Just to influence Rohan, Kunal asked the chai vendor "Who drinks more tea from my team?" The vendor replied "Praveen and Sameer sir, they were here sometime back."

Kunal: So who is going Onsite?

Tea-vendor: America?

Kunal: America!

Tea-vendor: Sameer sir is going for some work. He was saying Concert.. Vegas, something like that.

Both Rohan and Kunal were surprised as Rohan had no plans to send either of them to US on any project. They finished their tea and went back to office.

Rohan went straight to Praveen's desk. Praveen was busy attending some "conference call". He muted the conversation and told Rohan that he would reach out to him once the call is done. So Rohan went and started talking with Sameer. "What's up Sameer, how is work? Did you complete the task assigned to you?" Sameer replied that he was working at it. Rohan further asked Sameer "Hey I saw a leave request for 15 days from you? Are you getting married?" Sameer was slightly frustrated as he believed that life was more than work and marriage. But he kept his calm and replied honestly that he was going for a concert to "Las Vegas" where he was supposed to perform with a band. However it was not confirmed yet. Rohan could not believe that people could take leaves for participating in a concert and that too for 15 days. "Vegas is a fantastic place to be. I have been there couple of times when I was in the United States. Indians have amazing fascination for Vegas and they visit Vegas only to see the strip clubs." said Rohan. He laughed sarcastically. "We will see and it all depends on the task you have been assigned with." replied Rohan. "What is this quote? You seem to be too versatile huh. I seriously don't know how you work with so many distractions. You need to focus on your work dude. Guitar and music won't fetch you any money." said Rohan and left from there.

The news which Sameer never wanted to share was out. Rohan kept assigning tasks which were more difficult and time consuming. Few from Kunal's bucket too. He expected Sam to complete them all or perhaps he was trying to distract Sameer. Rohan asked Sameer to learn Automation. He wanted Sameer to ramp-up and finish the work assigned to him. Praveen was helping Sameer as much as he could. Sameer was about to deny the automation request but Praveen suggested him to accept the same and promised that he would help him. Sameer accepted Rohan's request to learn the same and automate few things before he left for his concert. Sam was arriving early and leaving late. Learning Automation was not a big deal for him as it was just a matter of learning the language and not the logic.

It was the first rainfall of the season, and everybody could smell the petrichor in spite being in an air-conditioned office. The drizzling rain drops were washing of the dried pigeon drops. Sam was terribly excited, not for the rains but for his dream turning into reality. In his excitement, he ordered sweets using the mobile app while he was still reading the email. "Sweets at my desk! I am selected as a Lead Guitarist for the BAND (EOM)." Everybody in the team walked to Sameer's desk and congratulated him including the Site head. Rohan and Kunal came too. Kunal congratulated with the comment "You are lucky man, you fetch money from everywhere." Rohan congratulated, but he did ask the status of the automation task.

Sameer was demotivated with Kunal's comment as he felt that money was least important to him than the opportunity to perform in front of huge crowd. He ignored the comment and got back to work. He realized that the leave he had applied was approved only for 5 days. Rohan had rejected his leave request for another week. Sameer had to discuss this with someone. He checked with Praveen if he was available. Praveen suggested him to talk to HR. Sameer was friends with HR and he felt that thy might help.

"Sameer, I think you should opt for "leave without

pay" or "work while you are travelling". You can negotiate with your manager, after all "it is at his discretion"." suggested the HR manager. "It is at manager's discretion" is a very frequently used statement by HR team. Sameer thought of discussing the same with Rohan. Neetu was at Rohan's desk and was discussing about the leaves she had applied for. She too had applied for 3 weeks of leave as she was supposed to travel for her friend's wedding to Jaipur. She was telling Rohan how excited she was about the "destination wedding" and the shopping she did for the same. In fact she had asked Rohan to Google the place where the wedding was happening. Rohan had his Facebook opened and was looking at Neetu's friend's pre-wedding photo-shoot pictures. "They are awesome Neetu, I think you should go. You should enjoy these times." suggested Rohan. Neetu said "I want to and have applied for leaves. But I have not completed my task yet." Instant came the reply "No worries dear, Sameer shall take care of your task. I have granted you 3 weeks. Please have fun and get me some sweets from Jaipur." "Yes or no SAM?" Sameer kept looking at the poster "Gender equality is a human fight and not a female fight" glued to Neetu's desk ☺ He opted to keep quite as he was shocked by the double standards...

The new automation project Sameer was working on needed him to collaborate with the team in US. Praveen suggested Sameer to talk to his team mates there and see if they have any suggestions. Taking leaves for 2 weeks, that too unpaid, was not working out for Sameer. Being a bachelor and on his own since his college days Sameer did not want his parents to pay for him. He came from a very well to do family which was why people like Kunal kept commenting "why would you need to do a job?"

Sameer dropped an email to the person leading the Automation project; he copied Rohan on the same along with the Site head who was also the part of the Funtoosh team. It read something like:

Hey Nik,

I have been selected as a "lead guitarist" for the band – FUSION (I am not sure if you have heard about it). Fusion will be performing in Las Vegas on 14th and 15th Feb. I will have to be in US for 15 days. I personally don't want the project to lag or delay due to me. However, looking at the task assigned to me, it seems difficult for me to do both of them together. I will be practicing mostly in evenings with rest of the team and I will be free in day time. But I will have to be in US. Would it be fine if I work from home for first few days and take leave during the show time?

Thanks,

-Sam

Rohan thought that Sameer was by-passing him in spite of Sameer copying him. "Sameer I know Nik and I am sure he won't agree with you." said Rohan. Rohan shared the incident with Kunal and Kunal as usual commented, "Sameer I am not hearing good feedback about you dude, I am glad I opted out to be your buddy" Neetu dropped at Sameer's desk, "Hey I will be on leave for a couple of weeks. Rohan has asked me to give you the TOI (transfer of Information) for the task completion." Sameer assertively asked her if it was an Automation task. Neetu said that it was not an Automation task. He dropped an email to Rohan saying that his plate was full already and he would not be able to help Neetu. This time, he copied Nik and Rohan's new manager. This aggravated the problem. Praveen suggested Sameer to hold until he got a reply from Nik. He was sure Nik would come up with the solution as Nik himself was passionate about music. Sameer desperately waited for Nik's reply. But there was a wait time of minimum 8 hours. And a lot had happened in those 8 hours. Next Morning, Nik replied, which read:

Hey Sam,

That's an awesome news and I am so happy for you. I am attending the concert to be held in Vegas as I am a big fan of the band Fusion. Also, you can work from home while you practice in evenings. Do not worry too much about work, Automation projects continue forever LOL.

Also, let me see what more I can do for you to make your stay easy while you are in US.

Rohan,

Please make sure you do not assign any other task than

automation to Sameer as of now.

Wish you all the best and we shall catch up in Vegas.

Thanks,

Nik

There was another email from Nik copying Sameer, Rohan, the Site head and Rohan's new manager which said, that Sameer need not take leave while he was in the States. Also, he said to bill them for his accommodation while he stayed there. Sameer was overwhelmed and he shared the news with Praveen. Praveen told Sameer that there was something more in store for him. Sameer was not able to guess what it would be. However, he felt as if Praveen knew it already and probably Praveen discussed it with Nik. He was speculating ... but was also rushing to complete his work. Rohan did not speak with Sameer unless he had some work to assign or status update to ask for. Neetu's task was now assigned to Imran who was on bench for past few months.

CHAPTER
Ten

"(2B ||! 2B)"

I mran was hired with Sneha and Sam as part of Amit's team. Amit was leading the QA teams and Rohan the Development teams. Kunal had moved from Amit's team to Rohan's team as he had good rapport with Rohan. In spite of the fact that Imran was in Amit's team, Kunal was asked to mentor him and for no reasons Kunal hated him from day one. Imran was technically very sound and a hardworking person. He hailed from Gujrat. His family used to stay in Gujrat and this person use to travel from Pune to Gujrat almost on every weekend which gave Kunal a kind of feeling that he would not be able to work on any task as he was not committed to work on weekends. Imran had three years of experience before he joined. Different people have different skills and can be good at one (and not all). Imran was a system tests guy. Good at testing the product as a whole. He was too good at handling different error paths. Ideally Praveen would have been a better person as a buddy for him, but when there managers like

Amit and Rohan, things tend to go wrong.

Being a bachelor, Imran would come to office early; around 8.30 in cab and leave late at his own will. He spent most of his time in office. His normal breakfast was a mug of milk from the vending machine installed in the office and more than a packet of biscuits from pantry. Generally, all the IT companies have their pantries loaded all the time with biscuits, fruits and snacks to munch on any time of the day. Lunches and other snacks are subsidized. Besides this, there are many other vendors inside and outside the campus. There is no shortage of food. Imran was a tall and thin guy. His size was not proportional to his appetite. Imran was a good painter and the only other thing he was passionate of was certifications in technology. It took time for him to learn things but once he did, it remained with him. Every technology he learnt, he made sure he was certified with that.

"Fix this defect in two days." said Kunal to Imran. That was Imran's first assignment. Being a tester, he could understand the defect and reproduce it but fixing it in the code was certainly going to take more time for him. Kunal asked him to go through the code in 1 day. He just gave him an overall view of the code. Whenever Imran had questions, he used to walk to Kunal and Kunal as usual replied "You don't know this? What did you learn in 3 years?" He would then comment, if he had to do it why would he ask Imran. That way he kept assigning task which were about fixing bugs, making changes in code. That was unfair said few of the teammates to Kunal. "Please mind your own business." was Kunal's reply.

Sameer was noticing this; he approached Imran on the internal chat to offer a cup of tea. Both Sameer and Imran left for tea. While sipping over the tea Imran asked Sameer if something was wrong with him (Imran) and asked him for his candid feedback. Sameer replied "Imran you are a great guy and everybody knows Kunal." "Then why is everybody so indifferent to me. Nobody wants to have lunch or snacks with me. In any party they would leave me alone. Nobody takes the same cab as I do. What is the problem?" asked Imran with tears in his eyes. "Imran don't feel bad. It will be better for you to ask him less and find out things yourself. You can check with anybody else but him. Don't get demotivated, we all are with you." replied Sameer. After that tea, Sameer walked back to office with Imran.

With that feedback Imran started learning stuff himself. He did try to learn and grasp ASAP (as soon as possible). But it was getting difficult for him. Hence, he decided to tell the same to Amit. In one of the meetings he told Amit, that he was not comfortable with Kunal. Ideally he should have said that he was not comfortable with the kind of work assigned to him. But... He was not aware of relation Kunal had with Amit. Amit took that personally and told Imran that he did not have any other work for him. So the only option Imran had was to work with Kunal or be on bench. Imran was frustrated overall and opted to be on bench, thinking that he would be assigned the right kind of work.

While on bench, Imran read a lot about the product. He kept on testing the product and made sure he was always updated about the technology and the feature changes. He would discuss a lot with Parag or Praveen or Sam. He kept on testing with the available resources and reported few defects. Unfortunately, these defects were marked as "invalid" as they were assigned to Kunal. He had a very cheap excuse to mark them invalid. "Since Imran is on bench, we cannot accept the defects." Amit had to intervene and tell Imran to stop testing while not on project. Sometimes product quality is at the stake because of big egos of team members.

Imran had nothing to do. Every day he came to office, gathered more knowledge and started giving presentations on technology related to work. Imran was becoming popular amongst all the employees and not just the team. In spite on bench, which is generally thought to be the honeymoon period, he made sure he was doing something that would "add value". He could have learnt table tennis or be a carom board champion or dump himself in the smoking zone. Whenever somebody was on long leave or there was a resource crunch, different manager picked Imran for completing work. He was able to cope up and complete the work. When there is nothing else to prove wrong, people get onto character of the person. Neetu kept a count on the number of mugs of milk he had, biscuits he ate or the number of apples he took while he left for home. Besides, she journalized the number of weekends he went home and how early he left on Fridays! There were many more things which kept spreading about Imran. Imran started feeling low and demotivated.

One of his friends from another team asked him to raise his voice by logging a "Mental harassment case", but he did not do that as he thought it would have a bad impact on those doing it. Imran had one question on his mind all the time "What was wrong with him, why was he not given any opportunity to work?" It was killing him internally. Not everybody likes being paid for free. People change their boss and not the job really. People change for the people in team and not the organization as such. Imran started looking out for job with other organization as it was more than 9 months. The good part he did during the 9 months times was, he logged everything he did and had most of the written communication. He had few very hopes, which was when he was assigned the task for completing the work Neetu was assigned. He thought that would be a good opportunity to prove himself again to Amit who he thought was very powerful at that location.

Neetu gave him the task list without much information as she was in a hurry for her friend's destination wedding. Imran, that time, was slightly aware of whom to approach and how to go about it. Being a system test fella, he put all his experience and knowledge he could. He filed as many defects as he could and improved the strategy in the time given to him. This time he made sure it was reflected at right places. "I cannot be political" was no more his statement. Neither was he political, he just made sure that he did the right thing. A lot of questions were raised on the work Neetu did while she was away. Of course, all her "khabris (informers)" communicated her about the happenings. As always, she reacted and called Rohan to save her life. Rohan was a little worried himself and could not speak much to her.

Neetu, cancelled her leaves and was back in office. She dropped an email to Imran copying Amit and Rohan

Imran,

Due to certain unavoidable circumstances, I had to cancel my leaves. I am now back in office and would like to take up the tasks I left you with. Please let me know the setups used and the task from which I have to restart.

Thanks,

Neetu

(There is only one religion, religion of LOVE)

Imran forwarded the email to developers with whom he was working on the defects he had filed and the person who was looking at the resources on bench. Imran was asked to continue with his work and Neetu was asked to continue with her leaves until further course of action was decided.

"Why did you forward my email?" asked Neetu to Imran. Imran replied calmly that he felt it was necessary for him to share the details with everyone. "Do they know that you bathe once in a week, why don't you tell them the same?" Imran had no clue of what she was talking about. "Bathe?" asked Imran to Neetu, "What do you mean by that?" "Correct! How would you know it because you don't bath at all? You don't even wash your clothes and socks." Imran was surprised and shocked as it was happening at his desk. A manager from nearby bay got up "Guys this is not a fish market, and we all are educated adults, aren't we? Can you guys use a conference room to vent out your frustration?" Imran was embarrassed and so was everyone in the team. Prejudices were out; she could not control herself and said many more things which are very inhuman. The fear of losing the job or insecurity of losing the work which she dreaded for years was seen.

Management of the people on bench was now handed over to the Director, who was recently hired and all the decisions were frozen. Neetu went on forced leave and Imran continued to work on the task for completion.

CHAPTER
Eleven

"When there is nothing to talk about,
they come down to Character."

-Anonymous

It was pouring heavily and almost 10.36 P.M in the clock when Vidya joined the weekly conference call

"Hello, am I Audible?" She was 6 minutes late and the call had already started. "How the F$$$ this broke? Who the hell checked-in latest? Fu$$$$ you all should test the code before you check-in." said the development lead. "Hello, am I audible?" repeated Vidya, yet no reply. Frustrated she logged off and logged in.

"Hi Vidya here, am I audible?" checked Vidya. "Yes you are. We have not started yet as we were waiting for you.", replied her manager, unaware of the fact that she had attempted connecting once. She was the only women in the team of 8 and perhaps the only women in that group. Her manager used to sit in the US office and was pretty impressed with Vidya's working style. That was the only reason for her to work on the on-going project rather than a sustaining project.

Most of the assignments/project/work outsourced to India offices are in the sustaining stage. Most of the initial work whether it is designing, planning or developing the product is carried out at the head offices or onsite location for service based orgs. When the product goes in its maintenance stage, the work is outsourced in China or India. To work on cutting edge, one has to be in head office. There might be certain amount of truth in the above few lines, but not completely as there are organizations that have their Research and development centers here. In either of the situations, a lot of travel opportunities are created. People travel across globe to get "THE WORK DONE".

While on call, Vidya's manager informed her that the senior executives were planning to visit the Pune office and it was expected from her to be the Point of Contact. Nobody knew Vidya until Leo's visit. Vidya was with the organization for 10 years. Perhaps the most experienced in that organization. Technically, very strong. Extremely ambitious, assertive and approachable. Most of the time she would be able to resolve the customer issues.

The entire program was planned by Vidya and Parag. Amit and Rohan had an hour's slot in this program. Just to co-ordinate well they all would seat in one conference room. They booked this conference room till the time visitors were around. Incase Jan and Leo needed something, they could simply drop down in this conference room was their thought while planning.

Everybody on the floor was informed about the customer visits. Whenever there were customers visiting, the entire team would go gung-ho about it. Preparation would start as early as a month. Power point presentation, and rehearsal for the demonstrations. Meetings, meetings and meetings. The floors are vacuum cleaned, the windows and the entire office is cleaned. Thousands of fresheners are sprayed (read exaggeration). All of a sudden the Air conditioners work in their full blown capacities. There is a sudden drop in all and everyone's temperatures

"Welcome"

Leonardo Fruze

(Sr. Vice President, Engineering, ABD)

Jan Fulich

(Vice President, Marketing, ABD)

Everybody in the office was excited. This is THE TIME when everybody wants to be in the "limelight". Everybody wants to at least have one meeting with the visitors. However, this opportunity is available to selected few. One has to be a pet like Kunal and Neetu or they really have to do something more.

Leo and Jan were coming for the first time to India. Most the offices in Pune would welcome the guest in Puneri style. They had Dhol-tasha, Puneri pagadi and Arti for them. It sounded a little unprofessional to few; however, Leo and Jan were overwhelmed by the gesture. Vidya introduced Amit and Rohan as a program coordinator to Jan and Leo. She explicitly mentioned that he should be approached for anything they needed. Instant came the reply from Jan "Vidya you will be our point of contact as we know you and Amit would be secondary." Amit took that statement to heart. All the meetings were going really well. They had plenty of questions for everyone. But the group was prepared to answer all of them. While everybody was having lunch, somebody asked Jan and Leo if they liked Pune. "Today is our first day and we have not got much opportunity. But we will try to explore few things today evening."

After all the meetings were over, it was around 4.30 PM when Jan asked Vidya "What places can we go and shop?" Vidya suggested few places to them, however she said "I stay very close to the city and I won't mind driving you there." They both were happy as Vidya was the authentic source for them. While leaving for the day, Rohan checked with both of them if they needed anything. "We are good and we will check with Vidya if we need anything." Yet again he felt humiliated. He along with Kunal left for the day. They went straight to the chai-tapari. While they were discussing few things, they saw Vidya, Jan and Leo leaving together. "When I asked them if they needed something they denied, and now they want to go with this lady. Don't know what is so special about her." said Rohan to Kunal.

That evening, Vidya took Jan and Leo to the down-town of Pune. Both Jan and Leo wanted to buy something for their families. They had heard of rich textiles and fabrics of India. Vidya took them to the famous Lakshmi road rather than a mall as she knew their interest. "These are the busiest streets of Pune and you can hardly find parking place here." said Vidya. "Almost similar to the market places we have back in New-York." replied Leo.

Jan: Hey Vidya, I have heard a lot about Indian ethnic wear. My daughter wants to have one of those. She has sent me some pictures; would you help me buy the same?

Vidya: Let me have a look at them.

She looked at the pictures and took them to a 500 square feet shop.

Jan: Oh this place really looks small, are you sure that you would get the same here?

Leo: Too stuffy. But quite a lot to see around.

Vidya: Trust me, you will get the stuff at right price unlike the bigger shops.

While they both were looking around, Vidya shared the pictures with the shop keeper who immediately showcased all he had in that category.

Jan: This is almost the same. What is the price?

Vidya: It is almost 100$.

Jan: That is cheap! Can I get 5 different of those?

Leo: I am thinking of carrying some for my daughter too. Hey brother one for me too.

The shopkeeper was excited. While his sales person was arranging for the required sizes, he ordered some Puneri snack and tea for them. Jan and Leo were having fun. The shopkeeper kept on showing and these guys were buying. After all the shopping was done, they gave the shopkeeper their international card. The card did not work and they were looking out for alternatives. They were feeling sorry as they might had to leave the stuff they bought which was when Vidya offered them help by giving her local card.

Jan: Hey Vidya that is big amount. Are you sure?

Vidya: Please do not hesitate. You can transfer me online.

They were obliged. "Indians are good at hospitality and you are the best example." said Leo to Vidya. Vidya blushed. She drove them back to the hotel they were put up in. She did ask them if they wanted to have dinner with her family. They could not say NO. However they said they would visit her the next day.

Next morning, Vidya was in before Jan and Leo came in. She was just going through agenda with Amit and Rohan for that day. Jan and Leo both came in with bunch of Indian currency. "Thank you so much for that splendid evening. We both enjoyed the time we spent with you,

here is the money." "Please do not mention, I enjoyed it too." said Vidya. Amit and Rohan had no clue of why Jan and Leo were giving Vidya almost 50,000/- Rupees. Jan realized the thoughts running through Amit and Rohan's mind. "Yesterday our cards did not work, when Vidya offered us help by paying through her card. We withdraw the cash this morning and are repaying her." "Oh ok." said in chorus both Amit and Rohan with a cunning smile on their face. That incident did not tail-ended there and was sold wherever possible at the price of Vidya's character.

After Jan's and Leo's visit, "Per evening 50,000/-" spread like a contagious viral. "Now we know how she gets her projects and blah." Vidya kept her cool and decided not to react. She too laughed at it when people spoke about the incident.

CHAPTER
Twelve

"Change is the only constant thing in this world."

Whenever it rains, the most affected areas are the roads as they are flooded with vehicles. It was a rainy morning, when Rohan called up Kunal to inform that he had left from his place and would reach his home in another 10 minutes. Rohan used to carpool with Kunal as they both stayed in same locality, the "Use less engery" practice you see. Rohan picked Kunal.

Kunal: Hi, Good morning. What is this early All-hands all about?

Rohan: (while concentrating more on driving as the traffic was driving him crazy.) I am not sure too, but we are going to be late.

Kunal: I can't believe that. If you don't want to tell, then say so (giggled).

Rohan: Nothing like that, but even we managers have less knowledge about the same.

Kunal: Are we going to have a layoff? How many resources? Is it me?

Rohan: Whenever there is an email with "REORG" as subject line, the first thing all the engineers will think of is "LAY OFF". Why? Why you folks are so insecure?

Whatever happens we have to take it with a pinch of salt.

Kunal: True that is☺. The HR email says "Introduction to Kiran Desai". Who is he? Do you know?

Rohan: No. I haven't heard of him.

Kunal: Let me check the "Linkedin" (Looks in his mobile Linkedin app). The profile does not have the picture. Linkedin should not allow people to create profiles without picture. But the profile looks very strong!

Rohan: Really? Check the FB.

Kunal: Okay. Let me do that. Nope, FB does not have it too. How disgusting it is!

Rohan: Must be some Gujrati man.

Kunal: Nope, "Desai" is a Maharashtrian surname as well.

Rohan: Is it so, I never knew that. Whoever it is, let the person be of our types.

Kunal: I swear. What is wrong with the traffic today?

Rohan: Ha ha, everybody from our office is trying to

reach on time.

Kunal: I know, otherwise nobody ever would turn up before 10.30 AM.

Rohan: Fuc$$$$ Why is this lady out of her car now?

Kunal: Looks like her car broke down.

Rohan: Ask her if she needs some help (winking at Kunal).

Kunal: Why should I? She seems to be of your age. Must be in her 40s. She will suit you more than me. You ask her.

Rohan: My buoy, love has no age... And even if she looks of my age. She is pretty good. Look at her! Fit and fine. The Saree looks good on her.

Kunal: That is what! Saree and the "Aunty category belongs to you" my buoy. But yes I agree she is beautiful, sharp features.

Rohan: I know your category fuc$$$$ (furiously). Let me ask her.

He rolled the window down and asked the lady "Do you need any help?" On that the woman replied "My car is fine, I have blocked the road on purpose, to help resolve the traffic. Please hold on till we have some solution." "Are you sure about that?" checked Rohan.

"Pretty much," replied the woman.

Kunal: I am not sure what she is going to achieve alone. But I wish if all our traffic cops were as beautiful and stylish as she is.

Rohan: Wow! Now she is stylish? Let us wait and watch.

Kunal: I wish we had that "Bhallal dev's chariot" from Bahubali.

Rohan and Kunal both laughed while sitting in the car and waiting for the signal from the lady to move ahead. Few localites got inspired by her and joined her to clear the traffic. Generally, ITIans like Rohan and Kunal do not have the time to get down from their AC cars and resolve the traffic situation. Exceptions like her are there. The traffic block was resolved and traffic was regularized. Rohan waved at the lady and thanked her for helping all. They reached office almost at 9.40 AM.

The reception area was all decked up with fresh flowers and notice board with a welcome note.

WELCOME

KIRAN DESAI

(Director of Engineering, ABD)

They both rushed to the meeting hall and realized the meeting was delayed as Kiran was late due to major traffic block. They then went for having breakfast, which generally is arranged with such All-hands. After sometime the HR announced to gather as Kiran was available. Everybody was trying to settle down when the HR started the All-HANDS. The HR then introduced Kiran Desai, who was the new Director of Engineering and was standing behind with her mug of coffee. Everybody turned around to see the new Director as that was the first time for all. Rohan and Kunal too turned around. They were surprised and shocked. She was the same lady who resolved the jam. They never expected "Kiran Desai" Director of Engineering to be a Woman. Both Rohan and Kunal looked at each other and smiled.

Everybody kept looking at the lady who wore a simple brown saree and a red dot on her forehead with her Identity card showing up. She looked like an unconventional leader. Quite Simple.

Kiran introduced herself as, "Well I don't have any presentation prepared for introducing myself. So to begin with, I am born and brought up in Mumbai and not used to Pune. We have recently shifted to Pune due to family needs. I have a Master in Engineering from Mumbai University and have completed my Management degree from Boston. I met my husband Pankaj there and we got married. We have three adorable daughters; two out of three are adopted. I have got total 18 years of experience most of them in Engineering and very less in Management. So you can ask me for any technical help. However during all my recent visits, I was told that you are technically very strong. I am against managing/supervising people as I believe in 'Live and Let live'. Being a Mumbaikar, I am very blunt and very assertive. My husband use to work in IT and in fact in this same firm before we left US. After coming to India, he converted himself from an Engineer => Entrepreneur. He is a Social Entrepreneur and works on providing basic facilities like TOILETS to less fortunate. I am very happy supporting him and very proud of the fact that his efforts are recognized at national level. He is a President award winner as a "Social entrepreneur". Apart from work, I love helping him and taking care of my family." Everybody applauded.

Kiran explained her vision for the growth. She continued "My track record emphasizes more on quality of work than the quantity or scale up. This is the first time ever I am hired for both. After joining, I had to travel to meet everybody we are supposed to work with. I have heard a lot about people like Praveen, Parag and I think recently it was Imran who created spur. It is so nice to see people collaborating with the counter parts. Many congratulations to Sameer. I am die-hard fan of music; let it be in any form. I think one should follow the heart and do what one is passionate for. My job here will be to facilitate and support everybody." Everybody applauded again. She further went on talking about the changes in organization and reporting. Amit and Rohan were now supposed to report her.

Some people carry a lot of positivity with them and the Air changed to "ALL +++". Everybody in the organization looked motivated. After the presentation was done, Kiran showed her family picture.

All the folks who were with the organization for longer time realized that Kiran was Pankaj's wife. Pankaj who referred Amit and who left organization to seek something which he wanted to. Amit was astonished as he knew a lot about Pankaj but was never introduced to Kiran. In fact, he did not know about Pankaj's marriage at all.

Amit: Hi Kiran!! That was such a wonderful introduction.

Kiran: Thank you so much!

Amit: So is "Desai" your maternal surname? As Pankaj's surname is different.

Kiran: That is true. How do you know Pankaj?

Amit: Hey! You know what? I was referred by Pankaj in this organization.

Kiran: Really?

Amit: Yes, in fact we were friends in school too.

Kiran: Really?

Amit: I lost touch with Pankaj after he left US and had the posting here in India.

Kiran: Oh is it?

Amit: I got too busy with my career and Pankaj with his.

Kiran: I have got another meeting lined up Amit. Catch you later.

Everybody disbursed; few with positive thoughts and few with negative conclusions. "She seems to be conservative. How can she wear saree to office?" said Neetu to Supriya.

Supriya: One should always wear branded formals to office. Is it not? That is why I always wear branded.

Neetu: Who puts this big dot on forehead to office?

Supriya: Ridiculous. And why would somebody build toilets, leaving an engineering job?

Neetu: Do you think she will be able to lead the team? She seems to be straight. For her role, somebody has to be very diplomatic and bureaucratic.

Lot of discussions, and lot of curiosity was floating around. "She is so versatile, and seems to be so generous. Her technical competency seems to be very high and yet she is very modest." While all this was happening, Kiran was busy meeting almost all the groups to know every person's skill. She had herself created an application which was to be installed on the mobile device. Knowing all her direct and indirect reports along with their skillset was a tough job but with this app, everybody could simply feed in their experience and interest.

She divided the existing teams based on their skillset and the work coming in. Everything was reorganized. Kunal and Neetu no more reported to Rohan. Neither did Supriya to Amit. Amit now had a complete new set of people reporting to him except for Rimsha.

Everybody now wanted to impress a single person and that was "Kiran" who was very hard to impress. In one of the effort to do so, Supriya who was leading the group and all women related activities in the organization arranged a "talk session with Kiran" where only female employees were invited. Kiran had her own style of working; she accepted the invite and insisted on 100% attendance. There were many women employees whom Supriya never spoke with or could convince them to join the session. She had around 9-10 out of 100+ women for the session. So she herself cancelled the event. Kiran asked Supriya "Why did you cancel the event?" On that Supriya said "Looks like nobody is interested." Kiran very casually replied "Not interested in me?" she laughed and left for the day.

Next morning, all the women-employees got an invite from Kiran's assistant saying "Let us know each other over the lunch. Get your tiffin boxes and join me for lunch." All the women employees were surprised ☺ having lunch with the Director was very exciting and most of the ladies accepted the request. In fact the room was full and they all had to shift to a bigger place. Almost all, except for those who were on leave missed the lunch session. In that lunch session, Kiran suggested that they would have elections for the post of "SPOC (single point of contact)" representing the women in organization. That was very welcoming rather than having Supriya who was a self-declared leader for that group. Kiran also sent an email that all the men should participate in the poll. So the Women Representative would be the one elected by Women as well as men in organization. Things were becoming transparent and more participative than dictated.

Kiran would have simply kept the role for herself, but she always believed in delegating powers to those responsible. Kiran used Polling for almost everything that required participation from employees. All the employee engagement activities were more fun as she announced the budget available in her meetings. All the travel opportunities were open and known to everyone rather than selected few. Things were moving on, oh no they were progressing. She now started accessing every person's performance rating given by the manager.

She had a lot of 1-1 with the members who were with the organization since long time. She suggested the HR team to amend the performance appraisals to have 360 degree feedback rather than just taking manager's feedback into consideration for her organization. Implementing the amendment was going to take time as it required some change in policies and approvals from the counterparts. For getting the same done, Kiran was supposed to travel to US yet again and that too for 1 more month.

CHAPTER
Thirteen

"If you are going to take credit for all my work, let me tell you about what I just did in the bathroom."

-*CT"

After the reorganization, Amit realized that he had Rimsha in his team too. Rimsha was with him for 4 years now. She was the only member from his older team and everybody else was new. Rimsha was fairly tall, and fat. Inspite of hard work, she could never grab Amit's attention technically and personally.

Rimsha had taken admission in the same gym as Amit. Apparently this gym was the most expensive one and was close to office. She cycled to office every day and was becoming an avid fitness freak. Rimsha would visit the gym during same hours as Amit. There was a dramatic change in her behavior and wardrobe too. Earlier she would be in office at around 10.30 AM or 11 AM and left as early 3.45 PM. Her boyfriend would drop and pick her from office. But for last few months, people did not see her boy-friend dropping/picking her. Hence people concluded that she broke up with him.

Amit: Rimsha, you are looking fit these days!

Rimsha: Really, Thank you so much Amit. Even you have lost your weight and tummy does not show up as much as it would earlier.

Amit: Yes, I have been working on the same. Anyway see you in office.

Rimsha: Yes.

Rimsha changed her office timings to match with Amit's. She would be in office before he arrived, as early as 8.00 AM and left after he did. She would pick any damn task which the team had to do. Amit was noticing this and was impressed by the change she brewed in herself. She grabbed every possible opportunity she could. She was picking more, doing less. Whenever Amit asked her to do something (it was Amit's habit to ask verbally), she would ask him to drop an email saying that she had a habit of forgetting things. Whenever she completed her task, she copied everybody in the team and someone from the higher hierarchy. Amit did not realize this for a long time as he was aiming for some bigger role. Besides that, he had started trusting Rimsha and was convinced that she will complete the work. They were interacting more. In office, in gym and sometimes in a café; close to office. But being mindful of the Sneha's experience, Amit was a little cautious this time and was not too eager to promote Rimsha.

Praveen was moved to another team and hence had to give the TOI to Amit's team. He was asked to complete a task with Rimsha. Praveen started working on his task. He almost reached out to everyone for researching on the task. He left no stone unturned and worked day/night. Rimsha, on other hand trusted internal repositories and the work done by earlier folks to help her finish the assignment. She forgot the fact that the task demanded something more. Rimsha noticed that Praveen was on the verge of completing the task. Praveen was a kind of person who would work, work and work. He really did not care for any promotion, money or recognition. Everybody knew he was a very helpful person and was often called as "Shaktimaan (One of Indian Television's Super hero)" by people who liked him. You ask him a question and he would go out of the way to help. Apart from his work schedule, he would find out time to help others. He had written 100s of document which would help the newer folks in the organization. These documents were not just technical but also on how to read pay slips, how to calculate tax or how to create setups. He was a consistent contributor to the technical blogs. He was with organization for more than 5 years and knew the in and out of it (technically). But because he was in Amit's team, he was still where he was 5 years back. Everybody said he had achieved "Nirvana" by not reacting on any of Amit's bureaucracy.

Rimsha would always work in silo and keep everything

secret as she would fear of somebody copying her work. If at all she had to ask for help, then she would ask Amit. Amit would then point her to someone else (as always). Rimsha, decided to check with Praveen as to where he was in his assignment. She liked what he was doing and asked him for help. Praveen, without having a single thought in his mind shared all the documentation he had done so far and left for the day. Next day, when he logged in, he realized that his document was renamed and edited with "created by: Rimsha". He was not surprised and did not care about it. Rimsha completed the presentation and everybody applauded her for her thought process. She did have the opportunity to thank Praveen for helping her out, but she evaded. "Thanks to all seniors in team for helping me out." said Rimsha while looking at Praveen. Everybody in the team knew that the work was done by Praveen, but nobody said anything. Nobody does. Everybody is busy in proving their own self and sprinting in the race of Number-1 position. Amit appreciated Rimsha for one more time.

Since then Rimsha was Amit's new "Supriya.. Sneha". She would share everything with Amit, especially the gossips. As Amit was now aiming for promotion, he was delegating most of the task to Rimsha. Getting the status from the team or ordering equipment. Instead of nagging the team members, Amit would ask the status of work done from Rimsha. She would then check with others and report to Amit. The only work she did was to accuse people, or verify the work done by them or pinpoint fingers at the work completed. Everybody in the team was cursing Rimsha as she had no authority and yet would nag people.

She was a very different person when she joined. So what changed her other than the boyfriend who ditched her? As a fresher when she joined with Sneha, she was assigned lot of tasks by Amit and she did complete the same timely on most of the occasions, yet the credit was given to Sneha. She and Sneha used to create lot of setups and hand it over to Amit. Whenever Rimsha suggested any changes or any ideas, they would be ignored. Next time Amit would pick the same suggestions and build on the same. Therefore, she thought of changing herself, including the work principles. Technically, Rimsha was a slow learner and would stay away from task, which required technical depth. Everybody in the team would finish multiple tasks and she would continue to work on the same task for weeks together. This she referred to as researching or digging in technical details.

In IT, the teams are distributed across the globe and everybody works in collaboration to get the work done. Rimsha never would ask for help from locals, Praveen was an exception. But she did not hesitate a bit when asking for the same from the people in remote locations. She would share her work with people remotely. This created a good Popularity rating for her amongst the remote colleagues. Amit was assigned new project, which required more collaboration and that became a plus point for her. Rimsha started projecting this as important co-ordination for project completion with the help from remote offices.

CHAPTER
Fourteen

"Travel for work fascinates, but work while travel does not."

-Anonymous

"Do you have a US Visa?" asked Amit to Rimsha. "I have my passport, but never needed the Visa." replied Rimsha. Amit dialed a number from his desk and said "Hey, can you get the Visa application processed for one of my team member? I am sending an email copying her; please process it as soon as possible since she needs to be in the States next month." Rimsha was speechless, and happy. She had shared her desire with Amit to visit the United States and she felt that Amit was helping her out with the same. "Happy?" asked Amit.

Rimsha: Of course!!

Amit: Please get in touch with the travel desk and they should help you with everything.

Rimsha: Sure.

Amit: Also, Parag is travelling with you. Please check

with him. He travels as much as he eats. Just kidding!

Rimsha: Who Parag? Oh yes! I know him. He had helped me in one my assignments.

Amit: Good you know him already.

Excited Rimsha left from there and walked towards Parag's desk. Parag was not at his desk. "Is Parag in today?" asked Rimsha to the person sitting next to Parag's cube. "Parag would come by 12.30." replied the man. "Oh that late? Isn't it too late to be in the office?" asked Rimsha. "That is his usual in-time. He stays in office till 1.00 PM almost every day."

"Oh, he seems to have a different working style." said Rimsha while looking at a few pictures on Parag's desk. They seemed pretty old. In one of the pictures, there was a lady in center with Parag and Praveen on her side.

"Who is she?" asked Rimsha pointing to the picture.

"She is Archana. Parag's wife and he is Praveen." said the person sitting next to Parag.

"Oh ok. Let me come some other time." replied Rimsha and left from there.

Onsite is a dream of every ITian and Rimsha had a burning desire to be there. In that project, she had to work from the US office location for couple of weeks. She was excited as that was the first time ever when she was getting an opportunity to be in the United States.

Parag, yet another senior member in the same organisation, was a frequent flyer for every customer problem. A person to be accounted for his debugging skills. Parag was never promoted by Amit for what he was. Parag hailed from rural part of Maharashtra, and had a typical dialect. However, he was able to convey whatever he thought efficiently. He had a very different working style and everybody called him "Don", incredibly independent and who never cared for promotions, or salary hike or perks. He was a WORKOHOLIC! The only thing he ever craved for was getting into details of the technical issue and helping the customer. That had made him clearly visible amongst all hierarchies.

Parag was with the organization for 5 years and more. He had started as a QA engineer with the organization. He had gained technical knowledge of the product almost as an Architect (not the one who designs a building, but the one who designs a product). He was known for his Design level defects and was a domain expert. In the tenure of 5 years, he had been to United States office at least 14 times, to the Europe and China offices at least 3 times each.

He loved travelling along with work, which was what made him eligible for all the customer issues. He would be ever ready to travel. Not that he was alone, he was happily married and had kids but yet he would travel even if it was for long time. He was married to Archana who used to work in the same organization and in fact in his team. Archana left the job after marriage as "husband and wife cannot work in same team post marriage". Everybody always wondered how she fell in love with Parag, as he was a completely unromantic person. Probably, that might have attracted Archana to him.

Archana, Parag and Praveen had joined the organization on the same date. All three of them had joined as freshers. Archana was hired as a developer. Praveen and Parag as QA Engineers. Archana, a good looking and multi-talented girl. Extremely resourceful, sincere and active in all extra-curricular kind of activities. She always carried that big smile on her face. Very good at classical dancing. Parag, Praveen and Archana always used to be together, be it for lunch or tea or some other celebrations. Praveen had proposed Archana for marriage, but somehow she got gravitated to that Mr. Imperfect/Mr. Wrong. She never worked after her marriage and preferred to be a housewife. In spite of being topper of her time in University and a bright Engineer, she opted to be at home. Which is what supported Parag to travel frequently. A better-half who took all the responsibilities at home and let Parag do what he loved to do.

Rimsha, kept looking out for Parag, but he was on a sick leave. Rimsha was travelling for first time. She was excited and equally anxious as she knew less about the procedures. She went shopping every brand she could. Leather jackets, handbags, skirts and something that she assumed people wore in US offices. When one is travelling for work, all the cost is incurred by the organization. Travel, stay and daily expenses.

Rimsha and Parag were travelling for 3 months, which is 12 weeks, hence Studio apartments was booked for them. Studio apartment; an apartment which includes a working kitchen, a living room and spacious bedrooms. Besides this the organizations do provide a rental car. Both; the car and apartment are shared, provided same genders are travelling at the same time. Otherwise if it is a woman and a man, they are provided with independent apartments and car. With current changes in our constitution, not sure if they would make any changes with respect to same. Driving in India and States is different for lot of reasons including the left and right. Yet, a lot of people prefer rental cars over cabs as they are definitely cheaper than hiring a cab like the Uber/Ola here.

Rimsha was slightly surprised when she read an email from travel desk while she was moving to the airport in the same cab as Parag. It read something like below:

Hello Rimsha,

Please take care of the following as you are travelling for the first time:

- *Carry your original documents.*
- *Carry medicines with prescriptions,*
- *Please use a body deodorant.*
- *Please carry a mouth freshener.*
- *Please carry enough washed and clean clothes.*
- *In case you plan to drive, please follow the rules.*
- *For anything urgent, please drop us an email.*

Thanks,

Travel desk.

"Ridiculous! Why would somebody send an email like this? We are adults. We understand all that." said Rimsha to Parag. Parag was busy on his laptop. Coughing, he replied "You are travelling for the first time. They will not repeat it. There are many people who don't follow that and everybody is in trouble." Rimsha was not convinced yet she smiled and went back in her thoughts.

This was her first experience at the international airport. Check-ins, security and immigration. It was a little troublesome for her to say that she was not going for training or work when asked by the immigration officer. She had rehearsed the same many times with Amit. Yet, somehow she managed it and got the stamp on passport. One of the major achievements in her life.

Both boarded the flight. Parag had his seat in the business class and she was in economy. She was a little uncomfortable as she was expecting to sit beside Parag. "How come you got the seat in business class? Why was I given a seat in an economy class?" asked Rimsha to Parag. Her inferiorities were peeping out. Parag told her that he too was booked with an economy class seat; however he upgraded himself to business class by paying extra money from his own pocket. "Oh! I can do that to while returning?" asked Rimsha. "Sure." replied Parag and walked back to his seat. Rimsha was restless as the plain was taking off. She was chanting beads when the flight took off.

Rimsha: Excuse me I tend to puke, can you please put me in the front rows if possible?

Air hostess: Sorry mam, you should have requested while checking in. Now we won't be able to move you. However, I can give you a tablet which will help you.

Rimsha: Oh. Ok. Give me the tablet.

Air hostess: Sure. I will get you one once we are stable.

Rimsha was not very happy, however agreed to wait. Later the Air hostess got her the tablet. She had the same and was soon asleep.

Air hostess: Mam, would you like to have your meal? She tried waking up Rimsha, but she could not. After 10 hours or so Rimsha was up. She was hungry, but the Air hostess had nothing to offer her in Indian Vegetarian meal. Rimsha's travel experience was not going as she expected. She was not allowed to walk-in the Business class where she could go and talk to Parag which was why she was feeling home sick already. She was not willing to talk to anybody else. She took another tablet from the Air hostess and dozed off yet again.

Rimsha, please wake up, we have landed said Parag to Rimsha as she was fast asleep and the Air hostess had failed to wake her up. "Have we, so soon? How come you are here Parag? How did they allow you?" asked Rimsha to Parag. She looked around. The plane was empty with just her, Parag and staff around. Embarrassed a little, she pulled her bag and started walking behind Parag. Thank you mam! Thank you Sir! Parag turned around to reply the staff and saw Rimsha on the floor. She had fainted, as she did not eat anything on the flight and had taken pills empty stomach. The staff moved her quickly to the first-aid room. After sometime, she was given some juice, which made her feel better.

The office cab was waiting for both of them as Parag had informed about the incident. It was a long car. While travelling from the airport to the studio apartment, Rimsha puked several times. Both the driver and Parag were worried. Parag was trying to make things lighter and trying to get her out of the sickness. He asked the driver to take them to an Indian restaurant which was several miles off the road. He knew that Rimsha would have many apprehensions about food. "Rimsha, I will tell you one secret to travel." said Parag. Rimsha was not too eager to take any gyan (prescriptions), however she did not have any option. "And what is that?" asked Rimsha. "You should be open to anything be it food, people and place. Anyway, we have reached the restaurant. Here we can have nice Indian meal. This is the only Indian restaurant in this area and closer to our office. We may come here every day for lunch/dinner." Rimsha was delighted. After some happy meal, Rimsha was now looking out of the car window. She was amazed by the landscapes, wider roads and disciplined traffic while the cab drove them from restaurant to the booked apartment.

Parag dropped her till her apartment and he left for his place. Upon reaching the apartment, she was surprised as it was beyond her expectation. The apartment was spacious, with a modular kitchen which included working OTG, microwave, refrigerator and Indian grocery. This grocery was stacked by previous B1 travelers. The living room was spacious with a set of television, a comfortable sofa-set and a clean carpet all over the floor. The living room had an attached balcony which had a lovely 4-chair sitting with a garden view. Unfortunately, there was no one in the garden whom Rimsha would speak to. She went ahead and checked the bedrooms. There were 2 bedrooms, both having bathtubs. The apartment also had a washing machine and a dryer.

Tired by the 18 hour journey, Rimsha just crashed and slept. When she woke up at midnight, she was scared. She was alone in that huge 2 BHK apartment. Even though she was used to staying away from family, she always had flat mates. She slept again as she had to be in office for a meeting at 8.00 AM. Next morning, Parag called her on the apartment landline to check if she was ready and wanted a lift to office. She was all set and replied in a yes. Parag had hired the car last evening after checking in the apartment. After all, he was used to it. They drove to the office which was around 7-8 miles away from the apartment. Rimsha was impressed by Parag's caring nature. They reached office in no time.

It was quite bright and sunny morning even if it was

just 7.00 AM. The office was surrounded by lush green trees. Huge parking space, well reserved parking spaces for the specially-abled, for the mommies to be, for the executives and then for the staff. The allotted parking space was thrice of the actual office built-up space. All the two wheelers, very few though, were parked on their main stands with helmets without locks.

Parag asked Rimsha if he wanted her to show the office. Rimsha had only one option and that was to say "yes". Parag opened the door using his access card. The security officer (mind you; not a guard) sitting at the reception smiled and wished them a "Good morning". Parag replied "Good morning" with a slight American accent. Rimsha smiled and was impressed again. Parag showed her the office and introduced her to the manager who she had to work with for next few weeks. She knew him on emails, but this was the first time she met him. With a very warm welcome and intro with the remaining team, he escorted her to the workspace she was allotted. A big spacious cube, which had 2 monitors, 1 server and a docking station for her laptop. The workspace had a nice welcome note. The manager explained her how to reach or approach the team members in case she needed any help.

"Hi! Good morning Rimsha, how was your travel?" asked one of the team members while walking with her towards the conference room where everybody was waiting for the Product Owner/Vice President. "Not as fascinating as I thought it would be." replied Rimsha.

The Product owner was technically a brilliant person but extremely blunt and upfront. He would not hesitate to abuse in case things didn't fit his bill. As everybody was updating, Rimsha was getting nervous as in the entire travel excitement she had completely forgotten about the project work assigned to her. She started looking out for emails and documentation sent to her. It was her turn, and she was blank. "Are you jetlagged? Do you have the plan on what you would be working on?" asked the PO. Rimsha was completely blank and she had no answer as she had not planned anything.

She replied, "I am preparing one and I shall update you tomorrow." "Were you sleeping, all these days?" said the PO. Nobody ever spoke to her like that, but such things do happen. "Get me the plan in next hour." said the PO and left for another meeting. Everybody in the team left including the manager. Rimsha kept looking for details, but the work was done by Praveen, hence she had no clue for presenting the plan. She tried and prepared something in haste, but that backfired. The PO asked the manager to help her or assign her some other work. She was moved from that project on the first day itself, which she was supposed to work on. This was very embarrassing. She could not call anyone, nor chat as everybody was out of reach. She left messages for Amit and Praveen to help her out in that situation.

While driving back, Rimsha was on the verge of crying when Parag asked her "How was your day?" Rimsha did not tell him anything and kept silent. Parag did get the details of the meeting that happened from the other folks. He invited Rimsha for dinner to make the situation lighter. They had dinner together and then Rimsha left to her apartment.

"How can he talk to me like that?" said Rimsha to Amit on the Skype call. "This is not the way to talk to a woman. I am thinking of complaining this to HR. This was so embarrassing Amit. Nobody has ever spoken like this with me."

Amit: Cool down Rimsha. That is the way he talks with everybody but he is a very cool person and a lot to learn from. Also, I had told you to prepare the plan before you left.

Rimsha: Yes, I agree I forgot in all the excitement. But...

Amit: Let me have a word with both of them and see if they can include you.

Rimsha: Thank you Amit. Good night.

Rimsha ended the call and got back to her emails. She kept looking for some more help from the internet, some local repository and other teammates. Meanwhile, Amit did speak with the stake holders. They were too stubborn about their decision and blamed Amit for not sending a candidate who was knowledgeable and prepared enough. Next day, Rimsha was assigned a new task on the condition;

if she was able to complete that task in next 2 weeks then she could stay in US for next 4 weeks or return home.

"I never went in depth. I should have taken efforts to understand the product details. Googling is not the option. This is becoming difficult for me. What should I do now." thought Rimsha. "I did take credit for Praveen's work and came here, but I should not have done that." said Rimsha to Parag when they were having dinner in Parag's apartment. "Rimsha, it is never too late to realize the mistake and act on it. You might want to mend it." said Parag. "I am thinking about the same Parag." replied Rimsha. Her thoughts kept multiplying leaving her restless.

The manager in US assigned her a buddy, for any of her technical queries. That was some help to her for sure. Rimsha started working with him. She would accompany him for lunch and snacks too. He made sure that she would reach office early and assigned her task on day-to-day basis. He insisted her to complete the task the same day, no matter how long she had to stay in office. That was becoming hectic for her. Somehow a week passed by."

CHAPTER
Fifteen

"Health is Wealth."

"Mom, is dad online?" asked Parag's son to Archana. "No not yet, I have tried calling him but looks like he is sleeping." replied Archana. "But it is Monday in US and he is supposed to go to office." "I know kiddo, but he must be busy with something. Also, he was awake for long time yesterday night." said Archana hiding her concerns. Archana kept calling Parag on his Skype and mobile. There was no reply from the other side.

It was raining heavily when Rimsha called up Parag on his mobile, she did not get any response. She called up on the intercom, and she was able to connect.

Rimsha: Good morning Parag, are you ready?

Parag: Good morning Rimsha. I was sleeping, give me 20 minutes and I shall be ready.

Rimsha: Parag, you sound tired. Are you well?

Parag: Yes, I am slightly unwell. But, I have one important meeting to attend today morning. Once that is done, I will return to the apartment and grab some rest. Looks like Archana called me too.

Rimsha: You should have taken some rest on the weekend.

Parag: I know, but I wanted to finish this project and lay hands on another one. Let me quickly get ready. Meanwhile please come in the parking.

Rimsha: Oh ok. Sure, I will be waiting in the parking. Few minutes later Parag picked Rimsha and they both drove to the office. "I will park the car and call up Archana. You can proceed Rimsha." said Parag while rubbing his hand over his chest. "Are you well Parag? You look really tired. Anyway, thank you for driving me to office." Rimsha picked her bag and started walking towards the office. Walking few steps, she realized that she had left her Identity card in the car. She turned around and started walking back towards the car. She saw Parag had collapsed next to the car. "Parag" screamed Rimsha as loud as she could. She ran to the reception to get some help from the security officer. The security officer called 911 and rushed with Rimsha to help Parag. In approximately 3 minute's time, the Ambulance arrived. Rimsha had tears when Parag was being carried to the hospital.

Parag a complete introvert, would continuously sit at his desk and would get up only for some chai or smoke. He had very few friends and would prefer to be alone. However, he would help each and every person who asked him for help. Rimsha was recollecting all the memories she had of him. They never spoke to each other unless it was regarding some work when in India. But in last few days, they had bonded quite well. They reached the hospital. Rimsha looked at the facility members and HR completing the admission procedure for Parag in the hospital. They requested Rimsha to continue with her work as they would take care of rest of the stuff. She returned to office with a sad face. It was traumatic.

Parag had his first Cardiac attack. It was a major one. It was so severe that it had paralyzed his right arm and right leg. While he was being treated, the doctors discovered that he had diabetes too which was delaying the recovery process. Doctors suggested the HR (Human Resource) team to inform his family members immediately as they had very less hopes for him.

"Hey is this Archana? Is this is a good time to talk?" asked the HR. "Hi, sure please tell me." replied Archana. "Nothing to worry, but you will have to travel to the States as there is medical emergency with Parag." said HR to Archana. "Is he fine, can you give me more details?" asked Archana. "Look, I cannot tell you more as I am not aware too but all the arrangements will be done by the organisation." said the HR. Archana could sense that something was wrong with Parag and they were hiding it from her. Parag's was a nuclear family. Hence, Archana was the only person to take care of the family. She gathered all the strength and dropped their two kids with her parents.

They had a 6 year old son and a 4 year old daughter.

Archana called up Praveen who was her only friend. In spite of whatever had happened between three of them, she was connected to Praveen and they shared good relation. Praveen knew about the incident already but was skeptical to talk about the same. He also told Archana that he was supposed to travel very soon for some other project work. She checked with HR, if they could club her travel with him as it would be a big moral support for her.

The HR was supportive and accepted the request. Archana knew that Praveen hated travelling and unless there was some emergency he won't travel. They left together from India. Archana kept weeping while she was on the flight. It was difficult for Praveen to console and he could understand the pain she was going through. Upon reaching the airport, Archana and Praveen were picked up by office cab. It drove them to the hospital directly. Both were tired and were dozing while in cab. Driver woke them up upon reaching the hospital and took Archana's signature for completing the trip. The facility and HR heads received Archana. They requested Praveen to continue with his travel, however Praveen wanted to see Parag once.

Both Praveen and Archana rushed to ICU. They had to go through sanitization as they were just out of a big travel. Archana was desperate to meet Parag. But he was in ICU, where no one is allowed. Visitors can only peep through. Archana collapsed on seeing Parag and just could not control herself. Unshaven and weak Parag was sleeping when Archana reached. He was alone and surrounded by big instruments. It was Parag's 3rd day in the hospital. She always saw Parag with his Laptop or mobile or simply lying around in house relaxing. Praveen felt extremely bad looking at the entire scene and left from hospital assuring Archana that he would always be there around whenever she needed him.

Archana checked with the doctors if she could take Parag back to India, as she had some support back in India. Besides, she was worried of the finances too. Doctors suggested that he should not travel, as it will be too hectic. However, they would decide in a week or so. They did indicate to her that they had less hopes and everything now was in the Almighty's hand. She could not control her tears, the HR team member present there consoled Archana and also told that Parag was covered under the health insurance and she should not worry about the finances. Everyone in the organization was willing to help her every possible way. That definitely gave her some relief.

Archana had to stay entire time with Parag and there was nobody else to help her. Even if Praveen was around, he had to work and it would have been too much of an expectation from him. However, Praveen did visit them almost every day in spite of his hectic schedule. On weekends, he asked Archana to rest and he himself stayed back at the hospital. He often got them the food he cooked at the apartment. The hospital did serve healthy food, but the magic that a homemade "Dal-rice" (Lentil soup served with rice) does, no other food would. He knew Parag loved the Indian food. He knew his love for sweets too. After all, they were good friends since long. Praveen would cook the dal-rice himself. The hospital staff would not allow them to serve Parag the food they got from outside even if it was home-made. However, both Archana and Praveen could pursue the staff to feed him home-made food once in a week.

On one weekend, when Archana and Praveen were having lunch in the hospital canteen, Praveen went in some nostalgia.

Praveen: What a flamboyant Parag was then, of course he still is."

Archana: Yes, he still is.

Praveen: (Became sentimental) what fun we had on that traditional day! Remember?

Archana: How can I forget? I still have that picture frame in my hall. "BEST DRESSED TRIO". I dressed up as a South-Indian bride and you both had worn the typical Maharashtrian Feta with White dhoti and kurta. You both looked so awesome.

Praveen: You looked beautiful too Archana. In spite of being a Maharashtrian, that South-Indian costume suited you.

Archana: Really?

Praveen: Of course. Just because you said, you both should click a picture on an Enfield, he purchased a Royal Enfield and he did all that to impress you Archana. He was (smiles with his eyes moist) madly in love with you and he still is.

She smiled with some tears in her eyes and hoped for Parag's speedy recovery. (After so many days Praveen could see some smile on her face)

Archana: Parag is just crazy. Once I just showed him an SUV of a friend of mine and described how good it was. Parag went and bought it the same day. He spent all his savings in that. We were not even dating that time. That was the first time I felt that he liked me more than a friend.

Praveen: I remember that, as I was the one who went with him for buying the vehicle with Parag.

"And you remember" said both Archana and Praveen to each other simultaneously. They both laughed. Archana insisted Praveen to continue.

Praveen: Archana, remember how Parag had proposed you.

Archana: Pretty much. I still have the pearl script on my hard drive. The script Parag sent printed "I LOVE

YOU" infinitely and would keep printing it till it was interrupted with a "YES" as a reply.

Praveen: Had the reply been no, your system would have crashed.

Archana: (blushing) I do remember after I typed a YES, it sent an email to Parag, CCed to entire DL (Distribution list) in India.

They both laughed again.

Praveen: I had coded that script for him, as he was too bad at it.

Archana: And do you remember the reply I got from the Vice-president on that email. He had replied that it was a "Design defect", how can a Developer say YES to a QA engineer.

Praveen: I know. He himself had filed a defect in Bugzilla with a summary "MISFIT FOR ARCHANA" and you closed the defect saying "WORKS FOR ME".

Both Archana and Praveen broke laughing so much that somebody had to remind them that they were in a hospital canteen. While they were laughing, the Doctor on duty called on Archana's mobile and asked her to rush to the ICU. Both Archana and Praveen rushed to ICU nervously. Looking at their sad faces, Doctor told them that there is some good news. "Parag has moved his right arm for the first time. And they now do see hope in him. It seems the home-made food cooked by a friend and the affection of a wife is working wonder than our medicines. We will move him out of the ICU." said the doctor. Archana could not control her tears and could not thank the doctor enough.

Parag was moved to a regular ward. Both Praveen and Archana were happy. After the staff completed the movement and everything was settled, Praveen embraced him and uttered "Get well soon man, we are missing you." Parag was still sleeping. Praveen left for the day.

Parag was recovering; Praveen now would get the home-made food every day as the doctor allowed to do so. He brought in food that Parag liked, after all Praveen was always the go2 person. Parag would wait every evening for Praveen desperately. He kept looking at the watch on the wall placed just opposite to bed. Praveen would leave early from office, go to the apartment, cook the food and pack it for all three of them. They all would have the dinner together. Praveen would then go back to office and finish the task for the day. Every day Praveen would bring up some "story" on the dinner table which took both Archana and Parag back in time. Archana and Parag were married for 7 years, but because of Parag's workaholic nature, they had lost the charm in their relationship. Archana never complained a word to anyone, even to Praveen as she adapted to it. Whenever someone asked her if everything was alright, she would simply smile and answer "ALL IS WELL".

With Praveen around, things were easier and Parag was recovering faster. He could now move both his arms and legs nicely. They had appointed a physiotherapist who would visit Parag twice and make him do some exercise. The doctors were fine with discharging Parag. Parag was now shifted back to his apartment. Archana felt better and extremely hopeful.

On a Friday evening, Parag was sitting with Archana in the bedroom when he started crying aloud. Archana was not able to figure out the reason. "Are you well? Is something paining? What is it? Tell me." asked frustrated and anxious Archana. She called Praveen who was busy with his assignment. Praveen told Archana that he will be there soon. Meanwhile, Archana kept asking. After crying for an hour or so Parag spoke.

Parag: You know what?

Archana: What?

Parag: You should have married Praveen. He loved you too.

Archana: Why are you saying this now?

Parag: You would have been happier with him.

Archana: How?

Parag: I always neglected you, kids and my own self. Work was my priority. You always reminded me of my health issue. I kept neglecting.

Archana: So?

Parag: You took everything on your shoulder and never expected anything from me. I am so sorry. I have decided that I will give you enough time.

Archana: Please forget all that and let us start over again.

Parag: Yes! And I want you to start pursuing your career again. I will take equal responsibilities at home.

Archana kissed him on his forehead and hugged him. The doorbell rang. It was Praveen.

Praveen: What happened Archana? Is Parag fine now? Why are your eyes moist?

Archana: I am fine. And Parag is fine now.

Both Praveen and Archana walked towards the bedroom. Parag with Archana's help stood up and hugged Praveen tightly.

Parag: Thank you for doing all this for me. I am the luckiest person to have a friend like you.

Praveen: C'mon Parag.

He kept patting Parag avoiding his tears to roll on his cheeks. But he could not control too.

Parag: I will take care of my health, Archana and Kids.

Praveen: Promise?

Parag: gentleman's Promise...

They all laughed and Archana quickly grabbed her phone to take a selfie for capturing that moment. "BTW, how is Amit's favorite Rimsha doing?" asked Parag to Praveen.

CHAPTER
Sixteen

"The harder you work, the luckier you get."

-Anonymous

Praveen informed Parag that Rimsha was moved out of the project as she had superficial knowledge about the feature. The work was assigned to Praveen and she was supposed to return. Praveen convinced the managers to let her work with him as he would help ramp her up quickly. Rimsha was now supposed to work on same project as that of Praveen.

Praveen: I want to help her, but I also want her to work for learning and not winning.

Parag: (Patting Praveen's back) this is one skill I love of yours buddy and I am extremely proud that you forgive the ones for what they have done to you. I know the way she took credit for your work.

Praveen: She is younger to us and has to see the world for herself.

Archana kept looking at both of them. She also told

Praveen that she had a call with the doctor and that the doctor said "Parag should be absolutely fine in another week's time."

Praveen: Wow! That is a great news. Even I will complete my work till then. Pune. Oh I miss you so much.

Parag: I know. We will celebrate our anniversary back at home Archana. By then we should be home.

Praveen: Oh yes. That's true. 14th Feb is just 10 days away. I did not realize. Let us plan something.

Parag: Sure. You let us know, we will do whatever you say brother.

Praveen: You both take care for now. I will see you tomorrow. Let me take leave.

Praveen left from the apartment as he was planning to go back to office and work. On his way, he called up Sameer.

Praveen: Hi Sameer! Are you busy?

Sameer: Hey Praveen. Tell me. We are all practicing, but we can speak.

Praveen: Do you want me to call later?

Sameer: Nope bro. Tell me. Anything for you!

Praveen: Is it possible for you to give me 3 passes to your show?

Sameer: Passes! You are my special invites. I will get

you the VIP passes. You just need 3?

Praveen: Yes! For me, Parag and Archana.

Sameer: Is Parag fine now?

Praveen: Yes he is. And he has anniversary on the same day as of your show. So I was thinking of taking both of them to Vegas.

Sameer: That is so nice of you. I will arrange for the passes. Just book your tickets and come down to Vegas. It is wonderful here.

Praveen: Sam. Remember this is a surprise.

Sameer: I will get you 4 passes. Can you also check with Rimsha if she is interested?

Praveen: Sure.

Sameer: I know she is a little weird. But she is really sorry about her doing. The other day she said, "I am ready to apologize to Praveen. But I don't know how to do it."

Praveen: She need not do that. I will check with her as she now works with me. Thank you. And please call me back. Don't get riveted in your practice. Bye and good night.

Sameer: Bye. Certainly!

Next morning Praveen went to Rimsha and asked her if she wanted to have lunch with him. While having lunch, Praveen told Rimsha about the plan. "Actually I want to come, but I have to finish a lot of work before I leave for India." Praveen told her that the concert was on weekend and anyways they would have to finish the work before that day. She was a little reluctant. Praveen assured her that he would help her out on completing the task. Rimsha finally agreed, on the terms of paying for her own flight tickets and stay. Together Rimsha and Praveen booked 4 tickets to Vegas. Praveen told Rimsha as well to keep it a secret. Sameer on the other hand confirmed that he had reserved few seats in the front row. Praveen was very happy about the plan and was equally pressurized as he was responsible for completing his own task, Parag's task and help Rimsha.

Praveen would leave to office as early as 6.30 AM, he would finish his tasks and then join Rimsha to help her out. Rimsha was taking time as she never went in the details. Later on in the evening, both of them would drive to see Parag and Archana. Parag was recovering. And Archana was realizing that Praveen was overloaded with work. She took some information from Praveen and started working on Parag's task. She knew about the technology and product very well as she used to work on the same. Their friendship was rejuvenating. And Archana was happy about the same.

While having dinner with Parag and Archana, Praveen asked "Archana I think you should start working again. Kids are grown up enough. Lot of things have settled for both of you. Not for money but for your own sake, what say Parag?" Parag responded instantly, "Yes Archu, you should work. You can start something of your own if you don't want to do a job." Archana looked at both of them, "Are you both crazy, who will me give job after taking a break of 8 years? Who will take care of this and who will take care of that. Parag is just out of bed. I don't think it will be a right thing to do." She kept on going with too many things. Parag and Praveen looked at each other and started laughing. "I know you were making fun of me." said Archana. Praveen told Archana that nowadays there are many companies who do give jobs to women who want to work after taking a long break. And considering the work she was doing, he felt that she should be able to cope up with the new job. Praveen asked her to update the resume and send it to him. "Praveen are you thinking of referring her in our company? We have crazy people in our office, you know it." verified Parag. Praveen did not reply and kept on doing what he was. There was something on his mind when suddenly he saw a "1-1" lunch request by Kiran Desai. He was surprised. He knew she was around, but he was unsure of her agenda. He had no other option but to accept. "Why would she want to meet me?" thought Praveen loudly. Parag and Archana both together said "Hmmm some good news." Praveen blushed, yet gave both of them an angry look.

Next day, it was almost lunch time; Praveen was working with Rimsha when Kiran dropped in. She checked with Praveen if he was ready to go for lunch. She also asked Rimsha if she wanted to accompany. Rimsha was reluctant, but Kiran insisted. She drove them to the nearby Indian restaurant. After reaching there, she could see the smiles on both Rimsha and Praveen's face. As just an idea of having desi (local) food overwhelms the mind while in a foreign land.

Kiran: How is Parag doing?

Praveen: He is better now and recovering.

Kiran: It is so sad to see such incidents happening with youngsters. Guys you need to take care of your health. Does he have his family here, who is taking care of him?

Praveen: His wife Archana flew here after the incident. She also used to work with us years back.

Kiran: Where does Archana work now? Has she taken leave for this?

Praveen: "Nope! She opted be to a housewife after their marriage. She is a University topper and a very intelligent lady."

Kiran: She does not want to work anymore?

Praveen: Not sure. But both Parag and I have requested her to consider working again. Let us see.

Kiran: I think I will visit Parag today or tomorrow evening, so will check with her.

Praveen: Oh that will be really nice of you.

Kiran: Rimsha how is automation going on? Is Sameer also part of the same project?

Rimsha: Yes, Sam has been in this project for few months. I was shifted after I came here.

Kiran: You should ask for help, there are people available to help. But you also need to make sure you give them due respect and credit. Everybody on the top can gauge who is doing what.

Rimsha was astonished. She looked at Praveen and was trying to figure out who reported the incident to Kiran. But both Praveen and Rimsha were surprised to know that Kiran knew almost everything. She was concerned of every single person who belonged to her organization. She further enquired about Sameer's concert and if they are going to the same. Praveen told her about Parag's anniversary surprise and also asked her to keep the secret. After the lunch, they drove back to office.

After coming back from lunch, Praveen got yet another 1-1 invite from Kiran. Praveen was clueless as he just had lunch with her. Taking in positive spirit, he went for the 1-1. Kiran was planning to create a team which would be specialized in creating technical documents and reference guides for customers. She had gone through Praveen's profile and found it fit for the team. Everything was already in place, but she wanted to refine it to have a better look and feel. In the 1-1, Kiran inquired about Praveen's aspirations. She checked with him if he was happy being in technical role or he was seeking any role in the management. Praveen had never thought about it as nobody ever asked him so. He told her that, he would think about it and let her know. She also told him the plan for documentation repository and if he would like lead that initiative. Praveen was very happy and accepted the request. "You have already completed your task, I definitely want you to help Rimsha, however, I would like you to focus on getting the documentation done." said Kiran. Praveen replied "I don't think Rimsha will be able to complete it on time." Kiran replied "I will be asking Sameer to join Rimsha after his concert is over. We will extend the stay for both of them by another 15-20 days. However, do not disclose about it yet to Rimsha or Sameer. I am still talking with the counterparts."

Days were passing by and Praveen felt he should disclose the 14th Feb plan to the couple. One evening when all of them were having dinner, Praveen said "What are you doing for your anniversary this weekend?" Both Archana and Parag were astonished as they both had completely forgotten about the same. "How do you remember about it?" asked Archana. "Well, I was the only person running around on a Valentine's Day, ditching my girlfriend (of that time), making sure everything is going fine." replied Praveen while laughing loudly.

"We have not decided yet, but let us see." replied Archana with a sad face as she knew Parag won't plan anything special. And being in an alien land, it will be difficult for her to manage too.

Praveen: How about Vegas, the place where we all wanted to go since ages?

Parag: I don't think it is possible Praveen.

Praveen: Why so?

Parag: Who would go with wife to celebrate anniversary in Vegas. Are you crazy?

They both had hearty laugh and Archana gave both of them a disgusted look.

Praveen: Anyway Parag, I hope you remember Sameer, the guitarist from our team. He is performing in a band called Fusion. They have a concert in Vegas on 14th. He has shared few front row tickets with us and I have booked the flight tickets 15 days back. I have checked with the doctors and they said you can travel now. However you should not sit for long time. The flight from this place to Vegas is hardly 30 minutes. Let us go man.

Parag walked towards Praveen and hugged him. "If you have planned it, then I am sure you must have thought over it. And I know you will not take any risk." Archana interrupted "Guys, I cannot come with you to Vegas." Praveen said "OK... don't come. We both will have fun. You sit in the apartment." Archana replied "Fine, I will join Rimsha." "Rimsha too is coming with us baby." said Praveen. "What? So you both will travel with her? And I will sit here alone? You always loved Parag more than me Praveen." complained Archana. Everyone in the room went silent for a minute as everybody knew how much Praveen loved Archana without even talking about it a single time. They all giggled again. "I have a ticket for you, it is you who don't want to go isn't?" said Praveen. Archana replied "You should ask me why you don't want to come Archana?" Both Praveen and Parag together "Why are you not coming Archana?" asked her and laughed again. Archana replied like most of the women would "I have no apt dress to wear." All three laughed yet again.

Archana: Someone's phone is vibrating.

Praveen: Oh yes it is mine. Why is Kiran calling me?

Archana: Please take the call, it might be something urgent.

Praveen: Hi Kiran.

Kiran: I was nearby the community you people are put up in. I was thinking of dropping by to see Parag.

Praveen: Oh sure. I am at Parag's place too. You want me to navigate you to the apartment?

Kiran: No worries. Just tell me the apartment number and I shall be there.

Praveen: It is E-8024.

Kiran: I shall be there in a while.

All three of them were surprised as nobody at that designation cares so much for people at the grass-root level. The door-bell rang and Praveen opened the door. Kiran had got some flowers with her which she gave to Archana.

Kiran: How are you Parag?

Parag: I am absolutely fine. I am thankful to God for saving me out of this.

Kiran: You should thank your friend and wife too.

Parag: Of course I am obligated to both of them for rest of my life.

Kiran: Who is taking care of kids back at home?

Archana: My parents. I left both the kids with my parents. They are missing school. However, I have informed the school about the incident.

Kiran: I can understand. Hope you take care of your health as well as Archana's health Parag.

Parag: Yes Kiran. It is a hard lesson learnt.

Kiran: Great. You all take care and enjoy rest of the stay while you are in US. I will take your leave. By the way, Archana we are having a "Return to work" hiring drive for women in March. Please think about it.

Archana was zapped. So were Praveen and Parag. "I will certainly think about it Kiran. Thank you so much."

Kiran: Take-care guys. Hey Praveen, Sam has sent me some VIP Pass and I may go watch his concert.

Praveen: Oh we all shall see you there.

Kiran: Looks like the cat is out, she winked at Praveen and left.

CHAPTER
Seventeen

"Thanks God it is A FRIDAY."

"Let us go for Happy hours people." said Kunal to Amit and Rohan when both of them were reading an email sent by Kiran. "Congratulations Sameer and All the best!" was the Subject of the email.

Kunal: Sameer is very fortunate man. He is going to perform in an international band while on leave from work. Plus a multi-national company like us is paying for his accommodation and musical tour.

Amit: Seriously. Plus the Site head is promoting all this.

Kunal: True. If we ask for an onsite, we are told that there is no budget. How hypocrite?

Amit: Sameer escalated the matter to team there; otherwise I had made sure that nothing would work for him.

Kunal: Since the time he has joined either he is in funtoosh meetings or doing something else.

Amit: Technically he is so capable that if he focuses just on work he will go miles. But nobody understands my views. He hated me when I was his manager. If I wanted to motivate him, I would have also put his posters. But why should I waste money? Come let us go and check if anybody else is coming.

The entire office was flooded with Sameer's event posters. Kiran made sure that everybody in office was aware of the "extra-ordinary" person. She believed that Professional life and Personal life cannot be separate. She always said that we cannot juggle between them, we have to integrate them. If you are happy personally, you will perform better in office and vice versa. Sameer saw Kiran's email before he left for his concert and he had no words to express his gratitude. He was highly gratified and motivated by her gesture. He replied her "Thank you Kiran" and left for the concert.

No matter how many emails are sent or who sends them, once people decide on "Happy hours" there is no looking back. Happy hours, which generally would start on a Friday early evening and finish as late as a Saturday morning. There was separate group for people going for happy hours. Most of the members in this group called themselves as occasional drinkers, and occasion can be every Wednesday, Friday, good news or sharing something that is hurting, conflict of interest with manager, and appraisal time which actually is a peak time. Folks from "Happy hours group" would leave office as soon as the

Friday bash would start or even after lunch.

Kunal, and Amit were pioneers of this group. Lot of discussions happen in this group, and at times lot of decisions are also made in this group. All the ratings for performance appraisals are speculated here and all beauties are discussed here. A very entertaining forum. In fact, so many product features and testing strategies are also discussed here. That is the reason why we see lot of bars and restaurants coming up. All the bars near the office areas are always full. Sameer also would be a part of this group, but since he had his concert he was not available for this one.

"You all think Manager is a Villain." said Amit sipping his glass of whisky and smoking some cigar.

Kunal: No no boss, I don't think you are a Villain. You inspire me and I aspire to be as successful as you are. Amit was overwhelmed.

Amit: Really, you want to be like me? Am I good? Thank you. It is only you, Suppu and Jagan who like me.

All the men on the table looked at Amit and asked "Boss who is Jagan and where is he now?"

Amit started telling more about Jagan. Before joining this organization Amit used to work with Jagan. Jagan was one of his colleagues and he was a very hard working fellow. He worked only for money. He always wanted to settle down in United States and worked for impressing the bosses there. One fine day, on Amit's recommendation, he was hired for a post in US team. He shifted with his family there. Jagan was the one who introduced Amit to alcohol.

After moving there, he worked for the company for a year or so. He later started applying in other companies and left the job. He now holds a "Green card" and is a Vice President with some company. He looks after projects outsourced in India and travels to India once in a year. After he left to US, he never spoke to Amit it seemed. "He exploited me." said Amit and had another sip. "Oh that is sad, but even you were in US, why did you come back to India? Otherwise you too would have got a Green Card." asked Kunal.

It seems Amit never wanted his daughters to be too independent. He wanted his daughter to complete their education and get married to some good men. "A woman should be like a woman, who would cook for her family and listen to her husband." were his thoughts for a woman. "I agree." said Kunal. "My wife is independent and she never wanted me to control her finances too. I opposed her doing a job, yet she wanted to." Kunal further added that they had a lot of conflicts. And his wife was staying with her parents for last 6 months. She had sent him a notice for divorce. "She does not like me spending time at work. Basically she is jealous of my growth. I really don't care and I am fine giving her a divorce. I don't want to stay with a strong headed and stubborn lady." said Kunal. Amit was surprised and so were others.

"Are you sure Kunal?" asked one of the men on table. Kunal was 3 pegs down, he very confidently replied "100%." One of the men on the table said "I think we need to respect our women, not just women but every human. Their parents spend equal amount of money on their education, they work hard to get those degrees and they too toil to earn that money which makes them independent. We should guide them and not control them. I agree that they should contribute, and if we are marrying, we should be committed as they are most of the time." To this Kunal very arrogantly replied "You keep your fundas with yourself." Most of the men from the group left. Only Amit, Rohan and Kunal stayed back.

"Forget all that people, there is going to be big change." said Rohan. "God knows what." replied Amit. "What is that Rimsha doing and how is that Parag-the super hero?" asked Rohan to Amit.

Amit told Rohan and Kunal that all of them had extended their stay by 1 weeks' time. Also, he informed that all of them were going to Vegas to watch Sameer's concert, even Kiran and Nik. Kunal was burning. He kept abusing Sameer.

Sameer's concert was on Saturday. Both Rimsha and Archana wanted to do the shopping as that was their last weekend in US. They requested the boys to take them for shopping. All of them were ready to go when Rimsha saw a message popped up. Rimsha had her office outlook configured on her email. She had got few "ship it" for the script she had posted for review. She thought that she could quickly check-in the script, so that she was then free to shop as long as she wanted to. Also, that was a very important script from the automation suite they were creating. Rimsha checked with everybody if they could wait for another 15 minutes and she would be back. She went back to her apartment and everybody waited in the parking.

She logged in to quickly "check-in" the script. She was able to successfully do the same. She left her apartment and was walking back to parking. Rimsha was staying in that community for more than 5 weeks now. The distance from her apartment to parking lot was just 2-3 minutes of walk. Parking was as lighted well. Rimsha realized somebody followed her. She was wanting to turn around but she did not. Suddenly she heard "Go back to your own country you XXXX-XX." This time she looked behind and realized that two tall men with a pistol in their hand were following her. They repeated the same statement again, pointing the pistol at her. Rimsha was scared to the hell and she ran towards the car. While she was running they did fire a bullet.

As soon as Parag and Praveen heard the firing, they came out of the car to see that Rimsha was running towards them. The strangers ran away on seeing Parag and Praveen. Rimsha hugged both of them tightly. She could not control her tears. Archana who was sitting in the car, was scared too. She consoled her as much she could. They were all concerned. However, at that point in time they decided to go with the plan as it was a matter of 5-6 days more in that community. After finishing their shopping, they all decided to stay in Rimsha's apartment and leave from there to Vegas as they did not want to leave her alone.

Next morning Praveen, Parag, Archana and Rimsha left for Sameer's concert forgetting the incident that occurred last evening. On the way to Vegas, Rimsha did drop an email to the HR manager who took care of the people on travel. Rimsha got an instant reply from the HR manager asking the details of the two men. Rimsha had hardly seen them but she did call up the HR manager and gave her the details. The HR manager had filed a case as a precautionary measure. The community they had selected was the safest one and had hardly seen any untoward activities.

CHAPTER
Eighteen

"What happens in Vegas, stays in Vegas."

-Anonymous

P raveen, Parag, Archana and Rimsha checked-in the hotel after their travel. All of them decided to rest as they wanted to prepare themselves for the evening. Rimsha and Archana were discussing few more things about the concert. Not everybody in the group was a big music fan except for Rimsha. Others were there to encourage Sam. While Parag and Praveen fell asleep, Praveen's phone rang. Archana picked the call, as she did not want to disturb the boys. It was Kiran who was boarding the flight to Vegas and wanted to check if they all had reached. "Would it be fine if I join you guys to concert?" asked Kiran. "Absolutely mam. As soon as Praveen is up, I will ask him to call you back." replied Archana. Rimsha and Archana were surprised as they did not expect Kiran to be there. She was supposed to be in another location on Monday. However, it seemed that she was dropping there as she was a big admirer of music and of course she wanted to see Sam. While the ladies were about to rest, there was yet another call on Praveen's cell. This time Archana had to wake him up.

"Hello is it Praveen? I am Nik. I wanted to check if you had few more passes to the event. Sameer told me to check with you." Praveen almost half-asleep replied "Yes we have lots, please come down. We are in Monte-Carlo, room number-5012. Call me again once you reach the hotel. To this Nik replied saying that they too were in Monte-Carlo and same floor. Praveen smiled and said "Seems SAM has a got a PR and fortune." Praveen took few of the passes and walked to Nik's room. Nik had come along with his family and he needed 4 passes. Nik introduced Praveen to rest of his family members. He mentioned to everybody that Praveen was one of the most hardworking and helpful person in the entire team. Praveen blushed. "See you in the evening Nik." said Praveen and left from there. Later on, all of them went out for lunch and visited few nearby places. They clicked a lot of pictures and selfies to upload on Facebook. All of them returned to the hotel as they were to get ready for the concert.

Kiran called up Praveen as she had already reached the place. Praveen asked her to come to the hotel as most of them were there and everybody could go together. It made sense to her. She dropped in at the hotel. She was able to meet Archana, Parag and Rimsha. She connected with Nik and family too. Everybody left for the venue where the concert was held. Entire road from the hotel till the venue had the Event posters put up. It was an open-air concert. The venue was closer to the hotel. The entire group decided to walk down to the venue so that they could see other places as well. Vegas is beautiful, rather more beautiful in evenings. Shimmery, breezy and full of energy. All the show girls, dressed in jazzy costumes dancing on road. Everybody wanted to click pictures with them. So did Rimsha and Archana. Both Rimsha and Archana were wearing the special costumes they had shopped. They clicked pictures at the known casinos, with the folks who were dressed up as renowned artist and of course all of them bought drinks for themselves in those tall glasses. All of them were excited when the "Fountains of Bellagio" played the renowned Hindi dance number. They were overwhelmed with the effervescence of the city. They kept walking until they saw a huge stage ahead at some distance.

By the time these people reached, the place was already full in the respective areas. The seats for them were reserved and very close to the stage. Kiran wanted to meet Sameer before the program and checked with Praveen if it was possible. Kiran called up Sameer and Sameer was very excited. He walked out of the backstage area and met all of them. Sameer also introduced his parents to rest of the group who were present to attend their son's first international concert. They looked equally proud as they would have when Sam graduated from IIT. Sameer was happy to see Nik. After meeting everyone he had to leave as they had to setup their instruments, however he promised to take all of them for Dinner. Kiran told him that she would have to leave early as she had her flight. "Next time.", said Kiran and patted Sameer on his back.

Vegas is a desert, yet it becomes very chilli in the evening. The entire place was lit up and it looked fabulous. The program started on time with the drummer playing the opening note. After a good opening, they slowly started introducing each band member. Sameer was third in the queue. As soon as he came on the stage, all of the guys applauded and whistled for him. Rimsha clicked on her Facebook live and was recording it. The entire crowd was enjoying the concert. It was around 8.30 PM when Kiran had to rush back. She informed Praveen and Praveen decided to escort her till the cab. He told Parag that in case the concert gets over by 9.00 PM, they should see him directly in the hotel or else he would come back at the venue. After seeing off Kiran, Praveen came back to the venue as the concert was not over yet. The band was asked to play more based on public demand. They continued for another 30 minutes and had to stop as they had some instructions from the security officers in charge.

After the show was over, the group could see a lot of fans approaching Sameer and his band-mates for autograph. Few of them were taking selfies. Sameer was a star by now. Flanked by beautiful girls around and few kids, Sameer was signing and clicking pictures. Media was around to click the pictures of their band. Praveen and group were waiting for Sameer to congratulate him. Both of his parents could finally get hold of him. His mother hugged and kissed him. His dad simply patted him on his back. Both Praveen and Parag hugged him. Perhaps hugging is the best way to applaud a person. And even better if you know them closely. It does not matter if they are just your colleagues. Rimsha and Archana told him that it was the best "Fusion" they had ever witnessed. Both of them clicked a selfie with the budding celebrity "Sameer". In fact, Rimsha tagged Sameer saying "Selfie with the STAR in making." Sameer's band-mates were requesting him to join for dinner. However, he told them that he wanted to spend time with his family members. Both Praveen and Sameer requested Nik to join them for dinner. Nik had other commitments; hence, he left after congratulating Sameer. Nik said "Sameer you were extremely cool with the GUITAR, as cool as you are while automating. It was flawless and entertaining. Superb performance by your entire BAND. I loved the way you had picked some Indian music with the western. Superb!"

All of them moved from the concert venue and walked towards the restaurant that Praveen had planned for. It was a special day. It was a party to celebrate Parag's Anniversary and Sameer's concert success. Everything was planned here too. While the dinner was being served, Praveen had ordered for a "Cake" with some "Champagne". This was a surprise for both Archana and Parag. And they both loved it. Sameer made it more special by playing their favorite song on Guitar. All of the others requested Archana and Parag to dance. Parag, a complete unromantic fellow did dance as the request was made by Praveen; a person who stood firmly with him through his thick and thin. He had too. They cut the cake and uncorked the bottle. All of them had dinner while sharing so many stories and discussing so many characters from office that wear masks. Different layers of human onions.

"God knows when they would remove the mask and realize their own self. Life will be so simple." said Rimsha.

REFERENCES

https://www.google.co.in/
search?q=best+quote+on+hiring&dcr=0&source
=lnms&tbm=isch&sa=X&ved=0ahUKEwjD1eDzuJX
XAhVk5IMKHce_B90Q_AUICigB&biw=1200&
bih=600#imgrc=3oGLdbCPkhl2YM:&spf=
1509266789333

*CT:https://www.google.co.in/search?q=cre
dit+taker+quotes&tbm=isch&tbs=rimg:CaiDos
y9OJLgIjgZLTk3gsJrDjlg_1WHSS-fkuBQqlB3o
CmIbVbWi6a7bnpbHn_1tyzlNd4g5sEByFXrtk
eY9RxjigUSoSCRktOTeCwmsOEUDgU4LTRu-
LKhIJOWD9YdJL5-QRS4hcSl4rr9IqEgm4FCqUHegKY
hHhoUuXMg5dHCoSCRtVtaLprtueEQt1QR6lnoOdK
hIJlsef- 3LOU10RkEZ9hT-Itk4qEgniDmwQHIVeuxFSv
jxbVt8wGCoSCWR5j1 HGO KBREZeTSRnxOSPN&tb
o=u&sa=X&ved=0ahUKEwirldnU5P
DXAhWLso8KHZSUARgQ9
C8IHA&biw=1200&bih=600&dpr=1.6#imgrc=G1W
1oumu256dxM:&spf=1512405645773

www.ingramcontent.com/pod-product-compliance
Lightning Source LLC
Chambersburg PA
CBHW031343170626
46807CB00002B/800